'From FBI studie[...]
the typical lustmu[...]
Babalino. 'He'[...]
twenties – and k[...]

'The FBI breaks lustmurderers down into two
different kinds, too, which may help us. First, there
is a disorganized asocial type. He is typically a
hermit, lives alone. He doesn't like people and
squirrels away in his house – he prefers his own
company. He has difficulty with personal
relationships and always feels rejected and lonely.

'The organized social is the other kind. He lives
among us. May be a student, a family man . . .
anything . . .'

TOM PHILBIN

A Matter Of Degree

SPHERE BOOKS LTD

A SPHERE Book

First published in the U.S.A. by Ballantine Books 1987
First published in Great Britain by Sphere Books Ltd 1990

Copyright © 1987 by Tom Philbin

Printed and bound in Great Britain by
Cox & Wyman Ltd, Reading

ISBN 0 7474 0284 1

Sphere Books Ltd
A Division of
Macdonald & Co (Publishers) Ltd
Orbit House
1 New Fetter Lane
London EC4A 1AR
A member of Maxwell Macmillan Pergamon Publishing Corporation

For Julie and Pete

ACKNOWLEDGMENTS

My thanks to Roy Hazelwood of the FBI's Behavioral Science Unit and to Jack Sturiano of the Suffolk County Medical Examiner's Office.

ACKNOWLEDGEMENTS

All you need is love.

—John Lennon and Paul McCartney

So we beat on, boats against the current, borne back ceaselessly into the past.

—F. Scott Fitzgerald,
from *The Great Gatsby*

CHAPTER 1

"Please don't tell Daddy."

Bobby Jo Johnson stood by the kitchen sink rinsing dishes. Her mother was sitting at a table behind her looking down, a pencil poised over a crossword puzzle. Bobby Jo took a little breath.

Her mother kept looking at the puzzle. She had a heavily lined face, a thin mouth, and white hair. She was thirty-seven.

"Why'd you fail?" Mrs. Johnson asked.

"Arithmetic's hard for me, Momma. I just can't seem to understand it anymore. I studied hard. You know, you saw me."

"Just how much?"

"At least an hour a day."

"I saw you study some. I don't know it was arithmetic."

"It was, Momma. I just can't get it. I just don't like numbers."

1

"You would if you studied more. You passed before."

Bobby Jo wanted to scream at her mother. She was such a bitch. But she couldn't. She swallowed the feeling. "I'll study harder, Momma. I will. I'll get it."

"Finish the dishes," her mother said as she filled in one of the puzzle boxes.

Bobby Jo did, rinsing and drying them carefully and putting them away. When she finished she stood near her mother and said, "Is there anything else I can do, Momma?"

Mrs. Johnson looked up. Her eyes were light blue, cold and flat, with little points of light in them. "Your arithmetic," she said.

In her room, which was on the second floor of the house where they lived, Bobby Jo lay on her bed. In her arms she held Sport, a teddy bear she had gotten one Christmas when she was three years old. She knew she was too old for Sport, but she held him anyway. He understood how she felt, and that made her feel better.

But Sport couldn't make it all go away. In the hour since she had talked with her mother, she had gone to the bathroom three times and still felt like going. She didn't know what Daddy would do if he found out she had failed arithmetic. But it would be something.

Maybe the shock thing. That hurt a lot. But it was better than being hit. Daddy could hurt bad. She had seen Momma with bloody noses and black eyes many times. He wouldn't do that to her. He told her he never wanted to mark her. She was his baby and the only thing that mattered to him in the whole world. He loved her.

Bobby Jo pulled Sport close to her.

"Oh, baby," Daddy would say. "Without you my life might as well stop. Once, your momma and me had dreams, but all the dreams went away, and you're the only dream that came true. You're all I got.''

So many times he would tell her he wanted to be proud of her—and she should be proud of herself too. She was to excel at everything she tried.

Bobby Jo did. At sports, at school, at everything; during the last couple of years she had virtually taken over the house from Momma, who started drinking as soon as she got up.

But now this. A failure. Momma showed her the failure notice the moment she came through the door. She enjoyed showing it to her. Bobby Jo had not seen Momma so happy in a long time.

Bobby Jo couldn't bear the thought, but Momma was almost for sure going to tell him. She loved telling Daddy about the slightest thing Bobby Jo did wrong.

But a few times she didn't. Bobby Jo remembered that at least twice when she had wet her bed her mother had not told her father.

Of course the discoveries had been made early in the morning, and by evening, after a day of drinking, her mother might simply have forgotten.

Please.

At around six, a cold hand slipped into Bobby Jo and squeezed. She heard Daddy's truck.

She got up from the bed and went to one of the two windows that overlooked the driveway. Her father, a crew-cut, muscular man with a big belly, seemed to Bobby Jo the biggest person she had ever seen in her life. He stepped out of his truck—he was an electrician—and then reached back into the cab and pulled out a package. Bobby Jo's heart soared—then sank. It was long and pink

3

with a yellow ribbon on it. She remembered that next week was her birthday. Daddy had gotten her a gift. He never forgot her.

Oh please, Momma, she thought. *Please.*

She stepped back into the room as her father slammed the truck door and headed for the house.

Downstairs, her mother had been watching TV. It went off a few seconds after Daddy came into the driveway. She heard her mother going quickly into the kitchen.

The front door opened, and her father came in. Bobby Jo went over to the bedroom door, which was open. She listened. She could feel her heart hammering.

Her father went into the kitchen. Her mother spoke.

The quiet was shattered.

"Goddamn bitch," her father screamed. "Just love to hurt me, don't you?"

Bobby Jo felt a cold wind pass through her. Momma spoke again, but Bobby Jo could not hear what she said. She heard her father go out of the kitchen, then to his bedroom. There was a silence for a moment, and then she heard his slow, heavy tread on the stairs. She moved away from the door to the far side of the room. She fought to contain the tears.

Her father entered the room. He had the notice of failure in his hand. He looked sad—sadder than she had ever seen him. She felt her eyes filling.

"Bobby Jo, you let me down."

Tears ran down her face. "I know, Daddy. I know. I'm sorry. I tried to study. I can't understand arithmetic. I just can't, Daddy."

"Oh my Bobby Jo, you could have."

Bobby Jo's head slumped. She thought her heart would break.

4

There was silence for what seemed like a long time. Finally, Bobby Jo looked up. Daddy was holding the notice of failure in two hands, looking down at it.

He looked up. "You know I can't allow this."

Bobby Jo knew.

Bobby Jo was in bed by nine o'clock. She held Sport tightly. The front windows were slightly open, and through them she could hear the song "Greenfields." It was making her feel sad, sadder even than before.

"Greenfields are gone now parched by the sun . . .
Gone from the valleys where rivers used to run
Gone with the cold wind that swept into my heart . . ."

Daddy was the only person in the whole world who loved her, and she had let him down. Oh, what would she do if he stopped loving her? Tonight he had seemed so mad, and sad. He had touched her with the wire from the battery more than he ever had. But she could take that. All that was left were little red dots on her arm. They would get better. But what would she do without Daddy? She squeezed Sport close to her. It was not a thought she could bear for long. It made her feel very scared and sad.

She thought of Momma and got a cold feeling. She could never remember Momma loving her. And she could never remember loving Momma. Only Daddy. Daddy and Sport. *Please, Daddy,* she thought, *don't ever stop loving me.* Tears ran down the sides of her face.

"Where are the green fields that we used to roam? . . ."

Light from the hall made her realize that someone had opened her door. She knew who. It was Daddy. She peeked over the covers. He was silhouetted in the door-

5

way. Her heart beat faster. He closed the door behind him, came over to the bed, and sat down. Bobby Jo could smell liquor. She didn't like that usually, but now she didn't care. Daddy was here. She was so happy.

"Are you all right, Daddy?"

"Sure, baby. How are you?" he said, his voice low and husky.

"I'm all right, Daddy. I'm just so sorry for hurting you. I'll try harder in the future."

"I know, baby," he said.

His breathing was short. He took her face in his hands and then leaned down and kissed her on the mouth softly. Then his mouth opened wide and his tongue went inside her mouth. She responded with her own tongue. She felt herself getting very excited, her breasts getting hard, her thing wet. She wanted Daddy very badly. It was not like in the beginning when it hurt. Now she enjoyed it and wanted to show him how much she loved him. Then they were together and she thrust her hips rhythmically up at Daddy. The bed squeaked as they did it, and she hoped Momma knew what was happening. She felt sure she did.

Bobby Jo was happy; waves of pleasure coursed through her. In the midst of it all Bobby Jo had another happy thought. The gift. Her birthday. Next week. She felt sure it was a dress. She had been wanting one, and she was old enough to wear it. After all, she was almost twelve.

CHAPTER 2

George Benton, a detective first grade in the Five Three, where the other cops called him "The Bent One," sat alone in his living room. The only light came through two windows that fronted on the street and from a dim yellow hall light.

The outside temperature had been around thirty when he went to bed, and the apartment had been cool. It was even cooler now, but the silk Ralph Lauren pajamas he had on were patched with sweat.

The nightmare that had awakened him was familiar; he had been having it off and on since he was a little boy, and he was forty-three now. But that didn't make it any less scary—plus this time it had a devious new wrinkle.

As usual, he had been running down a pitch-black tunnel pursued by an unfriendly gorilla. Also as usual, the gorilla had steadily gained on him, and the tunnel seemed endless.

Then, just as the gorilla was about to pounce, George

woke up, as usual, but this time to the terrifying sight of another gorilla coming through his bedroom window.

He lay in bed, frozen, as the gorilla, who had red eyes, advanced toward him. Then he really woke up.

It had been a nightmare within a nightmare.

George wondered about his heart. It must have been given a hell of a workout. He thought it was in good condition, but he should check to make sure.

He had the means to find out. Around his neck he hung a $150 top-of-the-line Sprague Rappoport stethoscope. He slipped the earpieces in his ears and auscultated himself.

His heart boomed in his ears. His eyes flitted this way and that until he was sure everything was okay: not a systolic click or venous hum to be found.

He placed the stethoscope in its case on a nearby table.

He took a deep breath.

His breathing was okay. Maybe he could chance a cigarette. He still had a pack from when he quit two years earlier. Cigarettes had a calming effect on him—except when he thought of the consequences.

That was why he had quit; that was why he would not smoke now.

All he needed, he figured, was one more puff. That might be the straw that broke the camel's back, a single drag the final insult to his bronchi (which had been insulted by smoke since he was fourteen); a death flower would form, the metastasis to the brain, and, as Thomas Wolfe had written, "the earth again."

Maybe he should take some medication. Just fifteen feet down the hall was a gargantuan medicine chest containing everything he could ever need. There was enough, as one squad member put it, to keep the Russian army in good health "during the siege of Stalingrad."

The custom-made cabinet contained, among other things, a basic CPR kit, a portable, battery-charged defibrillator, and a tremendous array of medications, including sedatives that could be taken orally, by injection, or by suppository.

George almost smiled. That was great. Got anxiety? Stick a Valium up your ass.

No, he would take nothing. When he was in Bellevue last year they had given him, at least at the beginning of his "stay," 8 milligrams of Haldol in pineapple juice. Great stuff. On that dosage he could have watched the *Titanic* go to the bottom with no more interest than he would have had in eating mashed potatoes.

He inhaled sharply. The anxiety was still there.

Of course there was one sure way to take the edge off it, but he had resisted that. It was childish, weak, and ultimately unsatisfying.

He felt his resistance crumbling.

Across the room was a TV set and, next to it on a table, a VCR. He picked up the controls from a shelf under the table and turned the machines on.

Soon Jane Fonda, dressed in striped sweats, appeared, all toothy, twinkly-eyed enthusiasm for the exercises she was about to lead. George watched her carefully. Jane Fonda exhorted him to begin. Filled with guilt, George began.

At five Benton was still sitting in the living room. The edge of the anxiety was gone—replaced by depression. Another dawn was coming up. In his life it seemed that he had seen a million dawns, and only a few looked pretty and promising.

Click.

He thought of his ex-wife, Joyce, and their eleven-year-

9

old daughter Beth. He had not seen or heard from either since June, when Joyce, Beth, and Joyce's new husband, Mort, had passed through the city on their way to Europe.

He had met Joyce and Beth by prearrangement in the Statler Hilton at nine A.M. and had taken them for breakfast. Joyce looked terrific, slim and sexy, a lot younger than thirty-eight. Beth looked good too.

They had a pleasant conversation. They seemed to be genuinely interested in how he was doing. Everybody smiled, talked, expressed how nice it was for everybody to see each other again. But Benton, who had often fantasized about them all getting back together one day, knew then that it was over. There was this vague yet detectable attitude—Benton caught Beth sneaking scared glances at him—underlying everything: They were talking to a patient who was destined to stay that way all his life.

Outside the Hilton they shook hands—this with a woman he had lived with for nine years and a little girl whose diapers he had changed and whom he dreamed about giving away one day—then Joyce and Beth got into a cab and he watched it meld into traffic. He could see their heads in the rear window, and they never turned around to wave, and he got this terrible feeling that they were escaping from him.

Enter the steel fist to grab his guts and pull everything out on the sidewalk. Standing there he had found himself unable to move, ready to do a fetal, the same way he did the day the lawyer called him in the squad room and told him, in declamatory tones, that Joyce wanted to divorce him. They had taken him, weeping and scrunched up, from the floor and put him on a stretcher, thence to Bellevue to get shock treatment four times a week for the next three months.

He did not drop, but he felt the justifiable scorn of people passing him by, sneering at him. His heart was hammering, ready to blow apart inside his chest, his blood pressure was in stroke country.

Somehow he got his feet moving, and after a few steps he realized where he was going: to the hospital. He would walk up to 68th and go into New York Hospital.

Of course there was another thing he could do. He could go home and take his wadcutter for brunch. But somehow he knew that, no matter what, he would never do that. Maybe.

Three blocks from the Hilton he found himself in a bar. He was drenched with sweat, and he quaffed two double Scotches as quickly as the goggle-eyed bartender could make them. It didn't handle the anxiety; didn't even touch it.

Then, an idea. Call his mother. After his father had died three years earlier she remarried, moved to Los Angeles, and became a realtor. God knows, he never felt close to her, but she was his mother. Maybe he could go to Los Angeles and live with her awhile.

He found a phone in the corner of the bar and dialed the number, which he knew by heart. Though it was only about seven o'clock California time when he called, there was no answer.

He had a thought: She knew his ring and therefore didn't pick up.

He was about to go back to the bar, or try to make it to the hospital, when he thought of Joe Lawless, felony squad commander and his boss. Benton just wanted to hear a friendly voice—or something—and though Lawless was one of the toughest people Benton had ever met in his life, he never laughed at weakness. Benton reached him at the

11

Five Three squad room, and it turned out Lawless had been looking for him. Lawless quickly filled him in: they had discovered the body of a little Spanish kid on a roof on Tremont and Webster that was reminiscent of the "Charley Chopoff" case in the sixties where little Spanish kids were showing up dead with their penises cut off. This kid was missing his penis too. Lawless wanted Benton to take the squeal.

Benton felt himself coming back before he hung up. One reason was the confirmation of Lawless's regard for him as a detective. Whenever there was a particularly difficult case, one where real investigative skills were required, Lawless would call on Benton. Sometimes, it was the only thing in his life that he could look at and feel happy about.

But there was another, darker reason that he never told anyone—particularly other cops—because they might think it was sick: He liked investigating murders, not grounders, but whodunits where the human toll was high, where the event would make the ordinary person's blood curdle.

For Benton, such cases were like Valium. Part of him would recoil, but part of him—a large part—would groove on it. It took him outside himself, away from the sad, scary, and depressing film clips that were his life.

In fact, he liked the whole subject of murder. Liked to read about it, think about it, talk about it. It wasn't as liberating as investigating murder, but it was enjoyable. And, of course, the more gruesome and shocking the material, the better.

His preoccupation had gotten him in trouble with Joyce at least once: she just didn't consider visiting Boston Strangler crime scenes a good vacation.

Benton cleared the case, which came to be known among

cops as "Charley Chopoff II" in a month. The uncle did it. Most of the detectives working the case—and they called in the hotshots from downtown—looked for a big pattern, more chopoffs; every detective remembered the original case. That was just what the uncle, who was "shtooping the kid," as fellow squad member Frank Piccolo put it, hoped would happen.

After fifteen years of homicide investigation that's the way Benton should have gone—but he didn't. He worked it like a regular homicide, meaning from the family members out, and caught the uncle in a couple of inconsistencies.

Benton had no idea why he had gone this way. It was purely instinctual.

Benton got up from the chair he was in and went across the room to one of the windows and looked down into the street.

It was typical of streets in the Bronx that still retained the look of the past, rather than the look of the present. There was no graffiti, no garbage, no rusted-out car cadavers. There were trees, leaves on the ground, a quiet, gentle scene. A still life from another time.

It was a scene, Benton thought, of utter desolation, and he slipped deeper into his depression. Maybe, he thought, he should pop an Elavil, say half a 75-milligram tablet. He knew that was not the way to go.

Click.

An image of Joyce waiting for him on some street corner in the city, him feeling so heroic, her big man . . .

Another image. With Joyce in the darkness of their bedroom, her telling him that his impotence didn't matter but his knowing that it did.

Another image: him, a child, waiting for his father to take him to the ballfield but knowing that he wouldn't.

13

He closed his eyes, opened them.

Mechanically, he thought of a squeal he caught three weeks ago. A security guard had wrapped himself like a hot dog in huge, multiple layers of polyethylene, a kind of Saran Wrap womb, with a scuba tube stuck outside enabling him to breathe. Then he had jerked off, but something had gone awry: He had come, but somehow he had lost his breathing tube; he had tried to cut himself out with a handy knife.

He didn't make it.

Image: Joyce crying, telling him, screaming at him how disappointed she was in him, how he had failed her. His screaming back that he hadn't, but knowing that he had.

His mind scanned and stopped at Albert Fish. He thought of the letter Fish had sent to Grace Budd's mother, telling how he had cut Grace up and cooked and ate her but didn't fuck her "thouh I couldve" and how the little girl's ass was the juiciest part of the meal.

The thought did nothing for Benton. He drifted downward.

Ha, he remembered, Noguchi the LA coroner sitting around with cronies on a boring Sunday and saying something that got him in big trouble: "What we need now is a nice plane crash."

Benton could understand that—and Noguchi wasn't kidding.

The phone rang. Benton froze. His mother had died, Joyce and Beth had had a change of heart and were at the airport, it was a crank call.

He went into the kitchen and picked the phone off the wall. It was Lawless.

"I'm on St. Bonaventure, top of Snake Hill. We got a bad killing here, and I need you to run it."

"What have you got, Joe."

"Woman. White. Looks like a dump. Decapitated—breasts amputated."

"Anything in her vagina?"

"There is no vagina. The whole vaginal vault is gone."

Benton said nothing.

"She's also bruised all over. I think bitten."

"Fifteen minutes." Benton hung up. He looked at the phone. He felt the pressure hissing out of him, like a punctured tire. Two minutes later he was in the shower, whistling.

CHAPTER 3

Twenty minutes later Benton was driving south on Webster Avenue. As usual, he was dressed in a suit and tie and overcoat—all bearing the Lauren label—and looked like a store model.

The car was a black 1984 BMW that he kept parked in a garage down the block from where he lived when he was home and in another when he was at the Five Three. Parked on a street near where he lived nothing would likely happen to it. In the Five Three, aka Fort Siberia, it would not last unmolested an hour.

He thought about Snake Hill. It was actually the crooked path of 178th Street that began at Webster Avenue and climbed very steeply to a dead end at St. Bonaventure.

Kids found the Hill great for sleigh riding. The previous winter one had been run over when he exited Snake Hill onto Webster.

It was, Benton thought, a street you would have to know about. Either live in the area, or research it real well.

Snake Hill was in an area of Fort Siberia that was south of Fordham Road, therefore in Death Valley, so-called by precinct cops because most of the city-leading 1.5 homicides a week occurred there.

Otherwise, there was nothing remarkable. Just a bunch of burned-out, abandoned buildings, almost-abandoned buildings, and mostly abandoned and burned-out people.

He turned off Webster onto 178th Street and climbed Snake Hill. Halfway up there was a small black man walking a huge German shepherd. Near the top there were three young Hispanics, a man and two women. One of the women was wearing a robe. They were hurrying toward St. Bonaventure. Benton turned right into St. Bonaventure and parked, then reached down and turned the Chapman lock.

The scene was at the end of the block. A big crowd had already gathered, and strobe lights lit up the sky; there was a cluster of blue-and-whites, red dome lights flashing. Soon dawn would be up and no lights would be needed.

He pinned his shield to his jacket lapel and walked slowly down the block. The street was flanked on both sides by apartment buildings, most red brick, but a few cream—or what had once been cream. There were five or six private homes.

At least five of the buildings had been gutted by fire. Most of the others appeared to be empty. At the far end of the block, he remembered, was an empty lot that let out onto a number of streets that zigzagged down to Webster.

Benton stopped, struck by it. It was unusual even for Fort Siberia: not a single building was occupied. The entire block was dead.

He started walking again.

A good place, he thought, *to kill somebody or dump them.*

Benton nodded to a couple of cops standing by a blue-and-white in front of the crowd.

He filtered his way through the crowd. He saw Piccolo and his partner Edmunton talking to some people. Getting anyone to talk if they saw anything would be another story. Cops were the Man.

The body was off to the right, on the sidewalk, shielded from the crowd by a makeshift white canvas screen and a blue-and-white. Detective Barbara Babalino, a beautiful dark-haired woman who was Lawless's fiancée, stood nearby, staring at the body. He could see Lawless's head above the top of the canvas screen.

The crime scene unit was already working the scene. Benton didn't see Vic Onairuts, the medical examiner.

Lawless came over and they walked to the body together. "Thanks, George," he said. "Vic will be here in about ten minutes."

Benton looked at him and smiled slightly. He nodded and smiled at Barbara. She smiled back. It had affected her, he thought.

Benton looked at the body. *It was,* he thought simply. *It was.* His face showed nothing.

He slipped on a pair of thin plastic gloves.

It was lying on its left side, the legs drawn up almost to the stomach, the arms looking as if they were clamping the body to keep it warm.

It was in a fetal position. Even without the head you could tell that.

You could also tell it was a woman even without the breasts and vulva. It had that certain symmetry.

Benton walked around it twice. Then he squatted.

There was little or no lividity, but there were bruises—bite marks.

He switched position so he could look up between the legs. A neat job.

There was a trail of dried feces going down the inside of the left thigh.

He went to the front of the body. The head had been removed neatly too.

He touched her upper arm. Still warm, even though the outside temperature was around freezing.

He bent the hands. Rigor had started.

She had not been dead long, maybe a few hours.

He got up, scanned and rescanned the body. He squatted.

He counted eleven small, red, crescent-shaped bruises, including one on the left buttock and another on the right that had drawn blood.

All were bite marks, probably ego cannibalistic variety. It took, he thought, a tremendous amount of pressure to draw blood with human teeth.

He stood up. The body was of a young woman. Benton guessed she was in her late teens or early twenties.

Something surged from deep inside him that, he knew, did not show on his face. Like the man said: She was too young to die. We all should live forever.

He circled again. No blood, except some near the neck and on the abdomen.

It definitely was a dump job.

"She can't be dead more than a few hours," he said to Lawless.

"Dump job?"

Benton nodded.

"She looks, from the wounds, like she was heavy in the chest," Barbara Babalino said.

"Maybe," Benton said, vaguely embarrassed because Barbara had big breasts, "but not necessarily. You can get wounds like that without a large chest. Who found her?"

"A derelict foraging for bottles and cans," Lawless said. "He's over there in the blue-and-white by the lot."

Benton went over to the blue-and-white. A uniformed officer who Benton only knew as Whitey was guarding him. Benton wondered why Whitey was standing so far from the car. When he got within six feet he understood. The derelict was ripe.

Benton went over to the man. "I'm George Benton," he said, offering his hand. I'm a detective with the Fifty-third Precinct."

The man was dressed in rags. His left ear was missing. He wore a cap that looked like it had been used as an oil rag. Benton saw the surprise in the man's eyes, then he put out a gnarled and filthy hand. Benton shook it.

"I'm Duke," he said.

Benton nodded. "You found the body, right, Duke?"

"That's right. I found the body. Me."

"Can you tell me how that happened."

"Sure," Duke answered. "I can tell you. I was in the lot looking for bottles and cans. It looked a like a good lot. No one had been in it in a long time. I found some bottles and cans—they're right here in my bag."

On the ground next to the open door was a green trash bag that looked like it had been used many times.

"Now, some of the bottles and cans was old, but that don't matter. I go to Pathmark. They have a machine that takes them. No hassle."

Duke's eyes were twinkling. He continued. "So I was just going through the lot and worked my way up to the street. I just kept goin'. I don't know why. I didn't expect to get nuthin' on the street. Those goddamn junkies get anything that ain't nailed down.

"Then I saw it. The body in the moonlight, as big as life. Knew right away it was a body, but something looked wrong so I went over to it. Then I saw it had no head and was all cut up. Scared me.

"I took off back down the hill. I didn't want nothin' to do with it. But then the cops in the patrol car stopped me when I came out of the lot, and I told them what I had seen."

"Did you see anyone on the street, Duke?"

"Naw, no one."

"A vehicle of any kind?"

"Naw, nuthin'."

"Well, thanks a lot for your help."

"You're welcome."

"Do you have a place where I could reach you if I had to."

"No," Duke said, "I'm between places now."

Benton reached into his jacket pocket and took out a card. He handed it to Duke. "You can reach me there if you remember anything else."

"When can I go?"

"Right now. Thanks again."

"You're a gentleman," Duke said. He got out of the blue-and-white, picked up his bag, and started to walk away.

The cop, Whitey, looked hard at him, then glanced at Benton. Benton's look told him it was okay.

Benton walked perhaps ten yards to the end of the street where the lot was. He watched the derelict go down it.

Benton went back to the body. Vic Onairuts had arrived and was examining it.

Lawless looked at Benton. "Anything?"

Benton shook his head.

Onairuts took about ten minutes to examine the parts of the body that were accessible, and then, with the help of an assistant ME, he turned the body over onto a vinyl sheet which had been placed alongside it.

Benton got down on his haunches and looked. There were three more bite marks on the other side, but none had drawn blood.

Onairuts spread her legs.

"What kind of a crazy would do this?" Barbara Babalino said.

Benton knew.

They watched in silence as Onairuts completed his examination and stood up. Two morgue attendants came over with a body bag.

"Any idea how she was done?" Lawless asked.

"Not really. I'll have to open her up first."

"How would you characterize the wound marks? Skilled?" Benton asked.

Onairuts nodded. "But not Johns Hopkins," he added.

"When are you going to do the post," Lawless asked.

"Later today."

Lawless nodded.

It went without saying that Benton, who headed the investigation, would attend.

CHAPTER 4

The last time there was an attempted robbery at Papa John's Diner at 183rd Street and Webster—in the heart of Death Valley—was in June of 1967, this after four successful stickups. It was an event that also hastened the end of hidden shotgun teams as a police tactic.

The perp, a black named Emmanuel Trombly, told the story of what happened from a bed in Fordham Hospital to two IAD shooflies. And the story was one of the favorites of cops sitting around getting shitfaced at any of a number of watering holes.

As Emmanuel told it:

"I dunno, man. I walk into the joint and put the heat on the dude, you know, and tell him to gimme the bread in the register. Well, he doin' that, you know, and then I hear like . . . like a noise coming from I dunno where, and the next thing I know somebody yell, *'Goobye muthafuckah,'* and the next thing I know I woke up here."

Perhaps that event, and the fact that there were always cops eating there, kept the bad guys out. Or maybe it was just because Papa John's was so run-down it looked like you could get ptomaine poisoning just looking at the signs.

Five minutes after they left the scene, Benton, Lawless, and Babalino were in a booth in Papa John's. Barbara and Lawless were sipping on coffee. Benton was sipping on a Perrier with a slice of lemon.

When they were settled Benton said, "You ever heard of a lustmurderer?"

"Vaguely," Lawless said.

"I did," Barbara said. "I saw some stuff from the FBI on them."

"That's right," Benton said. "Two guys from the FBI first profiled them. That's how I became interested."

It was, he thought, more than mere interest. He was mesmerized.

"I started to study them from there."

That wasn't so accurate either. Benton had collected everything he could that was written about them, and had made three trips to Washington to talk with the FBI about them. Plus, his last two vacations had been in lustmurderer country. He had spent one vacation in Salem, Oregon, where Jerry Brudos operated. And one weekend he had gone down to see where Albert Fish was born.

"A lustmurderer," Benton said, "could be defined as a sex killer and serial murderer. But he's—and I don't know a single female lustmurderer, except in fiction—differentiated from the other serial murderers in that he characteristically mutilates the female breasts and genitalia—or removes them."

"While they're alive?" Barbara asked.

"No," Benton said. "The doing is usually comparatively restrained. The victim's throat is cut, or a ligature is used. The real mayhem comes postmortem. Also the sex, if any.

"They're necrophiles?" Barbara said.

"Yeah," Benton said, "but not in the standard sense, usually. Typically, necrophilia means intercourse with a corpse, right? Here, the sex involves the use of a blade— the thing here is that the lustmurderer is preoccupied with destruction, postmortem mayhem with a blade. He likes to open the body up, get his hands in there, probe body cavities too. See what's going on."

"Yuk," Barbara said.

"Sometimes," Benton said, "there is sex, but rarely quote normal unquote. Sometimes they'll interact sexually with the wounds. Or masturbate onto the corpse. Usually, though, they orgasm when they're cutting the body or cannibalizing it. A number of lustmurderers were cannibals. Remember Albert Fish?"

"Yes, I've heard of him," Barbara said.

"He'd kill kids and defile them, and he told the guy who collared him that he orgasmed while he ate the flesh."

"Sounds like Jack the Ripper," Lawless said.

"The classic lustmurderer," Benton said. "Killed five women, didn't have sex with any, but ruined their genitalia and breasts—and a lot else. A cannibal, too, probably."

Lawless lit a cigarette. Two hours earlier Benton would have been worrying about secondhand smoke giving him lung cancer. Now he felt no apprehension whatsoever.

"Well," Lawless said, "who are the usual victims?"

"Young women. But little girls and boys too. The criterion is this destruction of sexuality of the victim, though sometimes a number of people are killed before the defilement occurs. Think blood, think postmortem mayhem—the FBI calls it post-offense behavior—and you're thinking lustmurderer.''

Benton paused. "For our purposes, though," he said, "we can work the case like any serial murder case, hetero- or homosexual."

Lawless nodded.

"I see a lot of similarities between the two," Benton continued. "The multiple killings, the way the killer fantasizes about killing, the need, I think, to challenge the cops. They also like to take away something of the victim. Here you have both clothing and body parts; it may be either: finger, toe, breast, hat, shoe—something.

"Now John Wayne Gacy was a homosexual killer, killing young boys, right? When they tossed his place they found graduation rings, wallets, lots of personal stuff owned by the victims."

"What the hell would they do with body parts?" Barbara asked.

A fleeting thought of Benton's: *Isn't this fun? The mind of the Bent One.*

"Different things. Sometimes they just hide them away. Jerry Brudos in Oregon made paperweights out of victims' breasts."

Barbara blinked.

"Sometimes they're used as sex aids. Edmund Kemper, who killed eight coeds around Santa Cruz, used to keep victims' heads wrapped in Saran Wrap in the freezer. Occasionally he'd take one into the shower with him."

There was a momentary lull, then Lawless spoke. "So he's going to kill again. The question is where."

Benton took a sip of the Perrier. "He may or may not kill here. Patterns vary. Ted Bundy killed in different states—wherever he was living at the time. William Heirens operated only in Chicago, and Henry Lee Lucas killed in twenty different states. Jack the Ripper worked only the Whitechapel area of London, the Yorkshire Ripper worked in a couple of towns, Dean Corrl—"

"Who's he?" Barbara asked.

"A homosexual killer in Houston. Killed only in Houston." Benton paused. "Whatever, I would say we should pull out the stops as best we can. Killing is, to maybe belabor a point, habitual with these guys. I don't know of one who stopped voluntarily. Heirens, they say, tried to stop but couldn't."

Benton paused again. "We're up against a clever killer, and most of them make it a point to learn police procedure."

"How?" Lawless asked.

"From TV, movies, detective magazines, wherever they can." Benton smiled. "But we know more—and we can narrow the search a bit. The FBI has started to track serial murderers with their VICAP program. Recently they started to feed their MOs into their computers. From all over the country. If this guy has killed before, he may be in the computer. And they've got a good profile of the typical serial murderer."

"Like what, George?" Barbara asked.

"He's usually white, young—in his twenties—and kills intra race. White kills white, black black."

"You think that's what we've got?" Lawless asked.

"I wouldn't bet against it. There's no great mystery to all this. It's statistical probability. A guy with this kind of a profile does this kind of crime. The explanations get elusive, I think, but of course we don't care about why— just who, right?"

Benton drained the last of his Perrier "I would also say that this killer doesn't look like one; I mean in the sense of looking like a drooling, wild-eyed madman. This guy could be a student, a family man, a minister. What's that Auden said about evil? Something like, it comes with a smile on its face and sits down to dinner with you. That's our guy. He's a monster living inside a human shell.''

"Nice," Barbara said.

"You pretty sure of that, George?" Lawless asked.

"Yeah, it's just more profile stuff. FBI studies break down sex killers into two kinds. They call one the disorganized asocial type. He lives alone, dislikes people, and though he does fantasize about killing, the actual killing is spur-of-the-moment. He spots a victim and does it, and the body is left as is.

"Our guy is known as the organized social type. The killing is all planned out. The victim is picked, and stalked and killed. And then, invariably, the body is taken from the scene where the murder occurs and dumped. Like here.

"Now," Benton said, "while this type of killer is slick, there is a process involved, a working out that leads to the murder. The killer was stalking, tracking, what have you—and somebody might have seen him at some point. The problem is that he's usually very careful. The disorganized type leaves everything but the kitchen sink at the scene."

The waitress came over and refilled the coffee cups of Lawless and Babalino. Benton declined another Perrier, though it occurred to him that he had not taken a leak since getting up. He probably didn't have diabetes.

"There are a couple of other things that may give us a better shot at him," Benton said. "One is that he may try to insinuate himself into the investigation. Serial murderers love to do that. For example, Kemper did that in Santa Cruz. The cops had a watering hole across the street from court, and Kemper conned his way inside. They just thought he was a big goof—but he learned about what they were doing.

"The other thing, and I'd say this is more likely, is that he will return to the scene to drop something off that he took from the victim."

"Why?" Barbara asked. "That would put him in jeopardy."

"I'm not sure. But one of the things about a serial murderer's personality is that they challenge a lot. Run risks."

"We can stake out the street," Lawless said.

"Right," Benton said. "Those houses make good spots. I would also stake out the cemetery, put a wire on the tombstone. The grave is a favorite dropoff spot of these guys."

"As soon as we have a grave," Lawless said.

Benton nodded.

"I can go with that," Barbara said.

Lawless nodded. "How many people do you think you'll need on this?" he asked.

"As many as you can spare. At least for the first couple of weeks."

"I'll see what I can come up with."

There was a pause while they finished their drinks. Then Barbara said, "Why do they do this, George? Why do they kill? I mean again and again."

"I don't know. It's curious, but in all the literature I've read, the answer is never really given. I have theories, but it's really a mystery.

"One thing is for sure: These guys all have horrendous childhoods. My feeling is that's where it all begins and ends for them. Not a single one was raised by Fred MacMurray or Robert Young."

Lawless and Barbara smiled.

And neither was I, Benton thought.

They went back to the scene. Benton was glad to see that his car was still intact.

CSU was still working the scene. Benton doubted they would come up with anything. Outdoor crimes were difficult enough in the country, where ground could record footprints, bushes snag fabric; in the city, finding evidence was even more unlikely.

But they had been able to take a few photos of the crowd. There was always the possibility, particularly given the profile of the killer here, that he could be somewhere in the crowd.

Benton talked briefly with Piccolo, Edmunton, and another cop who had been talking to the people in the crowd.

Nothing.

No brass had shown up at the scene, perhaps because of the hour. But Benton knew that eventually they'd get involved.

Benton left the scene and started to walk slowly down St. Bonaventure toward his car.

As he walked, he checked the entryways to each of the buildings, and in two cases the doors to dilapidated private homes. He was hoping he would find evidence of forcible entry, and then, beyond that, someone squatting in the buildings, and beyond that, someone who happened to be looking out of one of the windows at the right time and could remember something. It was a lot to hope for, and Benton knew it was unlikely that any of it would happen.

But he had to try anyway. You couldn't assume anything.

Along the way there were a few random collections of

junk on the street, and the yard of one of the private homes was fairly cluttered with junk.

Benton stopped at each pile and, donning gloves, picked it apart. He was looking for whatever.

There was nothing.

He came abreast of his car and paused. There were still some cops down the block. The car would be okay.

He started down Snake Hill, and as he did, he realized that the first few buildings on the block, both sides of the street, were empty. No one would have a view down St. Bonaventure. Yes, a good place for a dump.

Still, the occupants in the buildings should all be checked out. Maybe someone spotted a car going into St. Bonaventure between, say, midnight and three. What reason would a car have to turn into a dead-end street at that time of the morning? A lustmurderer would have plenty of reason.

Some of the buildings had garbage cans in front of them. Benton rummaged through them.

At one point he smiled. Even in Fort Siberia, some people must have been shocked at the sight of a man dressed in a Ralph Lauren suit picking at garbage.

On one of the blocks the buildings were separated by alleys.

Benton checked them and the garbage cans and bags he found there.

Nothing.

At Webster Avenue he glanced left and right. There were no garbage cans to the left, but there were a couple to the right. A black cat was on one of the cans, seemingly trying to get the lid off.

Benton walked over to the cans. As he did, the cat froze, eyed him warily, then jumped off and ran a few yards away. Benton opened first one can, then the other.

31

He probed the garbage with his stick. Nothing—but he did see the object of the cat's interest: a couple of strips of some kind of meat. Benton lifted them out with the stick and dropped them on the ground.

The cat waited until Benton was well beyond pouncing distance, then quickly scooted up, grabbed the meat, and scurried off.

Benton remembered. When he was a kid he had wanted to get a dog, but his mother and father would never allow it. It would mess up the house. Somehow, Benton could never bring himself to say he wanted it for company while they were gone on long, empty afternoons when the cold sunlight streamed through the windows onto the expensive rug and, somehow, made it seem even more lonely.

He walked back to Snake Hill and started up it.

He often wondered if people thought like he did. Everyone else in the squad room would talk about such mundane things: their lawns, their homes, their beer, their children, their pensions—that was a biggie—the PBA, and on and on. He was always preoccupied with destiny. His destiny, the destiny of everyone. He wondered why people did this, why they did that. Even killers. Particularly killers. He wouldn't show it, but he would always wonder what confluence of events had occurred in someone's life to bring him to the moment when he killed someone. Or, like the serial killer, killed repeatedly. What would bring a human being to the moment when he got sexual pleasure out of butchering a dead body?

Other cops would have simple answers: They killed for drugs, or a woman, or to advance a business position, or, as Frank Piccolo, once put it, "Because they're fucks." But Benton was never satisfied with such answers. The real answers were different. And one thing he knew, as he had said to Barbara: It all went back to childhood. Serial killers were children first.''

He thought of Ken Bianchi, the Hillside Strangler. When he was a little boy in Rochester his mother used to discipline him by holding his hands over a gas burner.

And Bundy. He was illegitimate. He was born in Philadelphia and was shipped out west because his mother and her family were ashamed of his illegitimacy. What could that have meant to Bundy when he found out? What else was a parent like that capable of?

And Fish. When he was five his eighty-year-old father died, and exactly one month later his thirty-two-year-old mother put him in an orphanage.

And Kemper. When he was a little boy his father strangled his pet chicken and then made him sit down with the family and eat it for dinner. Kemper said he cried for days.

And Henry Lee Lucas, who confessed to killing 300 people but probably only killed 150. He had a father who was a double amputee with no artificial legs who used to drag himself around the house like a snail, and a mother who was a prostitute who used to dress little Henry Lee up like a girl and make him suck off her clients before she serviced them.

The bizarre thing, Benton thought, would have been if these people didn't turn out crazy. That's what they were: crazy, all of them. Never once, Benton thought, had the childhood failed to show a severe problem between child and mother. There was no question that the killer was killing a symbol of his mother— what psychologists called the surrogate mother—who many times actually resembled the killer's mother. But that still didn't explain why. What did killing a symbol of his mother do for the killer? Benton could never figure that out clearly. You could say revenge, rage—but it still wasn't enough for Benton.

And what of me? Benton thought. He had spent his life feeling weak, anxious, and insecure, and hiding behind various images. Like being a cop. That was one reason why he had become one. He could step into a ready-made tough-guy role.

He knew that it was back there in his childhood. When he had been hospitalized, he had talked with an old psychiatrist who really impressed him, a Dr. Stern—which was not descriptive of the man at all—who said he thought he could help Benton, that together they might be able to get to the bottom of his problems.

After he got out of the hospital he had gone to Stern for a couple of months, but then had quit, something that Stern had sort of predicted: "We will explore childhood events, and you may find that very difficult."

At the time, Benton didn't think so. But he had to assume it had some validity later. It was the only thing that explained why he quit. And why he hadn't returned. As bad as he felt, as tough as things got, he did not pick up the phone and call Stern. What kind of terrors could his childhood hold? He wasn't Kemper or Bundy or Lucas or Fish.

He remembered a lot of things that, at the time he experienced them, he knew had scared him. But when he thought about them now they didn't seem to bother him. They just presented themselves in his memory, and that was that.

He remembered how, when his mother and father were out of the house—which was most of the time—and he was alone, he used to be so afraid of the sounds in the house: the gurgle of plumbing, the whirring sounds from other apartments, sounds he could not identify, that he would imagine some fearsome thing breaking into the house and getting to him. He used to go into a closet with his toys and stay there quietly so the monster couldn't find him. But he no longer *felt* that fear, it was just a memory.

Still, he knew the answers were there, and, ultimately, he knew why he didn't pursue them: He was afraid. Too weak, too insecure to probe. Whatever had created him had made him too weak to solve his own problems.

Still, somewhere down deep inside himself he could sense an ember. Maybe someday he would go back there and find out what made him what he was. And at the very same time he realized that the longer he didn't do it, the harder it would be.

Benton reached the top of the hill. He looked down St. Bonaventure toward the scene.

What made you, lustmurderer? he thought.

CHAPTER 5

Steve Rogers stood on the corner of 196th Street and Briggs Avenue, outside the Swanson's Sweete Shoppe, where everyone gathered. With him were Ray McCatlin and Tony Indelicato, who, like Steve, went to St. Mary's Prep. Unlike Steve, they were not three-letter athletes.

Whenever he could do it undetected, Steve glanced through the luncheonette window at the big electric clock over the fountain area. Almost eight. Time was running out. Where the hell was she?

McCatlin and Indelicato knew, of course, that she was supposed to meet him. He had made a point of telling them.

Rogers sucked in a little breath. Always, in the past, he never really worried about a girl showing up. But he worried about Bobby Jo Johnson. He had never seen a girl as beautiful or as well built. Thoughts of her had sent him into the bathroom quite a few times.

He had first spotted her in gym class, and the sight of her made him go hollow-sick in the stomach. *God*.

36

Later, when he found out she was not yet fourteen, he couldn't believe it. He didn't care. He wanted her. He was very relieved when she seemed to like him.

This was to be their first date.

Christ, if she didn't show he would be very embarrassed. To be stood up by a thirteen-year-old girl. Just to be stood up by a girl. McCatlin, Indelicato, and a whole lot of other guys would get on his back and not get off.

But, jeez, he just wanted to be with her. When she looked right at him with those big brown eyes he really had to work on staying cool.

Five after eight.

Where the fuck was she?

McCatlin and Indelicato were talking about a hot new book, *The Carpetbaggers*. Rogers made believe he was totally involved. He wasn't.

At ten after, McCatlin asked, "Hey, Rogers, where's your girlfriend?"

"Who the fuck knows," he said. And thought: *I should have picked her up at her house. But she said no, her father was funny about boys.*

Jesus.

Steve froze. There she was, coming diagonally across 198th Street.

He felt something crawling in his stomach and balls at the same time. Sweet Jesus.

McCatlin and Indelicato stopped talking.

Bobby Jo was very conservatively dressed in a white blouse and tan skirt, but she couldn't hide it. Rogers wanted to yelp with joy.

"Here she comes now," he said huskily, and thought, *You unlucky fuckers!*

She came up. She smelled like a flower store.

"I'm sorry I'm late," she said. "My father wanted me to do something for him."

"No sweat," Rogers said. "It's not dark yet. They don't start the movie till it gets dark."

"Oh good," Bobby Jo said.

"See you later, guys," Rogers said, and he led Bobby Jo toward his customized '53 Chevy across the street. He couldn't resist a backward glance. McCatlin and Indelicato looked green.

A half hour later, Bobby Jo and Rogers were sitting in his car in the Whitestone Drive-In watching *The Creature from the Black Lagoon*.

Actually, Rogers was having trouble concentrating. Even in the half darkness and looking straight ahead up at the screen he could see Bobby Jo's tits, and he wanted to grab them.

But he hesitated making a move. She was, he told himself, so young. He had never fooled around with someone that young.

And maybe her father was a nut. Come after him with a gun.

In fact, though, Rogers knew what he was going to do all the time. He was in the driver's seat, and his right arm was draped across the back of the seat, and his fingers touched Bobby Jo's left shoulder.

Gradually, his face still fixed on the screen, where one worried guy was talking to another worried guy, he moved his hand downward, superconscious of any resistance. There was none, and soon he had his entire hand over Bobby Jo's breast—or most of it; even his big hand couldn't cover all of it.

He squeezed.

38

It was firm, very firm, and for a disastrous moment he thought it might be a falsie.

It wasn't. Falsies didn't come with nipples.

Playing it cool was over for Rogers. He turned Bobby Jo's head toward him and kissed her—and got a surprise.

She immediately slipped her tongue in his mouth and probed with it.

Thirty seconds later, another surprise. Bobby Jo's hand was on his thigh, then she had grabbed his penis through the fabric. She stroked it a few times, and then Rogers felt her hand undoing his belt, zipping down his fly.

Her tongue continued, throughout, to probe.

He could not believe what was happening. She was incredibly hot, almost scary. Expert.

She pulled free of his mouth and, with his help, stripped his pants and underwear down to his knees.

Through a haze of lust, he was aware that he should fix it so he couldn't be seen by people going past the car, but he did nothing. He didn't want to risk stopping what was happening.

Bobby Jo leaned over. The pleasure was the most intense he had ever experienced in his life.

Two hours later, after a drive down from a heavily wooded area of Van Cortlandt Park in the north Bronx where they had gone after leaving the drive-in, Rogers dropped Bobby Jo about four blocks from her house.

"I can take you all the way. No problem," he said.

Bobby Jo, standing next to the driver's-side door, looked very serious, almost sad, a far cry from the wild, crazy person in the woods who had left Rogers feeling like he weighed four pounds.

"This is good," she said. "I'll see you at school."

Reluctantly, Rogers nodded. He watched her walk a little way. Then she turned and waved. Rogers waved back.

She was unbelievable. He couldn't wait to tell Indelicato and McCatlin about her.

Bobby Jo walked two blocks before she stopped under a large tree that shielded her from the view of most of the houses on the quiet block.

Carefully, she undid the beret holding her long blond hair up and let it fall down to her shoulders, then she combed and brushed it out. This done, she took a small jar of cold cream from her pocketbook, spread a thin layer on her face, and then wiped it and her makeup off with tissues. She threw the tissues on the ground and started to walk the rest of the way to her house.

Bobby Jo inhaled sharply. If Daddy ever found out she had gone out with a boy he would be very mad. He had told her he didn't want her to see anyone until she was twenty-one. Momma had gone into the hospital for drinking, and Bobby Jo's place was in the home.

Still, it had been worth it.

Bobby Jo had been noticing boys for a long time now, and she had noticed Steve the first day of school. He was playing basketball in the gym. He was tall and well built and handsome, a real hunk.

She had decided right away that she would have him, and she knew she could. For a long time now she realized that boys were always admiring her, and sometimes men. A couple of times she had caught old men looking at her.

She "accidentally" ran into Steve a couple of times, and then she noticed, though Steve didn't know, that he was going out of his way to meet her. The first time he talked to her he acted super-cool, but she could see that there was a little vein in his neck that was beating very fast.

Steve had been great. Bobby Jo felt very good. She knew she had pleased him.

The hollow feeling came into her stomach again. At one point she was going to have to tell Daddy that they couldn't make love anymore. She liked other boys. What they were doing was wrong. She had been thinking about that for some time now too.

She wondered what Daddy would do if she said that.

And what would he do without her? The thought made her sad. She was all Daddy had.

What would he do? She didn't know, but she knew she was entitled to her own life. A life with someone like Steve, maybe, where she could raise her own family.

She would tell Daddy how she felt the first chance she got.

She really would.

When Bobby Jo turned the corner she was disappointed to see her father's truck parked in the driveway of their home. And outside in the street near the driveway was a car she had never seen. It was big and had high finned things in the back. It puzzled her. Who owned that?

She went up the path that led to the front door. On the way she looked through the bay window into the living room. She could see her father—the back of his crew-cut head—sitting in one of the chairs. Across the room from him was a TV, which was on. Bobby Jo went through the front door, which was unlocked, and through a short foyer. She stopped at an archway that led into the living room.

Daddy did not look her way. He had a brown quart bottle of beer in one hand.

41

"Hi, Daddy," Bobby Jo said. She went over and kissed him on the cheek. The smell of the beer was strong. He didn't respond when she kissed him.

Then he looked at her. His eyes were bloodshot.

"Where you been?"

"To the movies. You know."

He took a long swig of beer. A little ran down his chin. "You're late," he said.

"Me and the girls went to a luncheonette after. I'm sorry."

"What'd you see?"

Bobby Jo was ready. She had seen it a week earlier. She knew what it was about. *"To Kill a Mockingbird."*

Daddy said nothing.

"G'night, Daddy."

She kissed him again. Again, no response.

She was almost out of the room when his words stopped her.

"You're lying."

She turned. He was rising from the chair.

"What?"

"You're a lyin' bitch. You didn't go to no movie with your girlfriends. You went with some punk to a drive-in."

Bobby Jo blanched. She had the feeling that she was her mother. She had heard Daddy talk like this to her mother a hundred times.

He moved toward her, weaving. He was going to beat her, like he beat Momma.

He stopped a couple of feet from her.

"See that car out there? I followed you in that. Followed you and that punk to the drive-in, then to the park. What'd you do, you little slut, fuck him? You was there an hour when I left."

42

The words came out of Bobby Jo before she could stop them. "That's my business! What I do in my business!"

Bobby Jo saw stars, then realized she was falling. She hit the carpeted floor hard.

He stood above her, quaking with anger.

She started to cry, but beneath the tears was something else: rage. "My business! My business! My body! You leave me alone from now on. I'm not going to let you have me anymore!"

Then he was on her, straddling her chest, grabbing her hair with one hand. He slobbered. The smell of alcohol was intense.

"You don't tell me what you're going to do. I tell you. I tell you!"

Then he started slapping her. He hit her ten times before he stopped. She was almost unconscious. He was breathing heavily.

"Now you get your whore ass upstairs before you really make me mad."

And he hit her one more time with a closed fist. She could taste her blood.

After she came out of the shower, Bobby Jo looked at her face in the mirror. Her mouth was swollen, and both her eyes were blackened.

She had been crying in the shower. Now she started to cry again, her mouth pulling back in a grimace over bloodied teeth.

Now there was no one else in the world for her. She felt so alone, and what could she say at school? Everyone would ask her about her face. She would have no explanation. She would have to think of something. Or she could skip school, just play hooky until she started looking a little better. In the meantime she could think up a story to tell.

Later, in bed, she listened to Murray the K. on the radio. Every now and then she would cry.

She thought of calling Steve, or maybe going over there, but he was just a kid like her. There was nothing he could do.

She thought of Momma. She remembered that Momma used to look like she did. She cooked for Daddy, she cleaned the house, she was his lover, and now he beat her just like he beat Momma.

She clenched her fists. No, no, she wouldn't let that happen. She would leave the house first. But where would she go? Where? She thought about that a long time, and then she fell asleep.

It was the smell that awakened her. The smell of alcohol. Daddy was sitting on the bed with her. He had his hand on her neck.

"I'm sorry I had to hurt you, baby, but you got to know what your place is in this house. Okay?"

Bobby Jo said nothing. She wondered if Daddy could see her eyes filling with tears in the darkness.

Daddy stood up and started to strip. He had taken off his shirt and undershirt when she said it. Softly but clearly.

"No."

"What?" Daddy froze.

"No. No. I told you. No more! I'm not going to let you love me anymore!"

She waited for the explosion. There was none. He was looking down at her, but she could not see his face in the darkness.

He turned and left the room. She didn't know what he

was going to do. Maybe nothing. Maybe he wouldn't try to bother her. Maybe she had told him. Maybe . . .

She tried not to be afraid. She could feel the beating of her heart. She had almost thought he wasn't coming back when he did.

She sat up. He had things in his hand.

He came up to the bed. "On your stomach."

She stayed immobile.

He dropped something on the floor.

He was on her then, his powerful arms turning her over. "You little slut. *I* tell you what you're going to do. *Me.*"

He pulled her arms roughly behind her. She wanted to cry out—but to who?

She felt tape being wrapped around her wrists, binding her hands together. She could see a box on the floor. Cotton.

"Leave me alone," she sobbed. "Leave me alone. Or . . . I'll tell on you."

"You will, huh? You will?"

He increased the ferocity with which he was wrapping the tape around her hands. Then, just as she was about to scream, he covered her mouth with tape.

He ripped her nightgown off. His pants came off; they fell in a heap near the cotton.

He picked up the cotton. What was he going to do?

Violently, he stuffed a lot of it in her behind.

Thirty seconds later Bobby Jo was screaming into the tape.

Later, he cut the tape and told her he was very sorry but she had to learn a lesson. He was her father, he was head of the house, he decided what was best for her, and he didn't want her to go out with any more boys. She was still too young.

Bobby Jo agreed to everything.

She spent the night holding Sport close to her, crying intermittently.

The next morning, as usual, she made breakfast for her father. Before he left at seven-thirty he told her what he wanted for supper, as he usually did.

"You okay, baby?" he asked before he went out the door.

She told him she was fine.

Then he left. Bobby Jo watched him through a living-room window. He got in the truck in the driveway, backed out, and pulled away.

In that moment, she realized that the man driving down the street in the red truck, growing small in the distance, was someone she had never really known.

She turned from the window, and she felt like weeping. It was as if, in that moment, her father had died. What was left was the man in the truck. And he would never touch her again.

Fucking never.

Three hours later, Bobby Jo was on a bus rolling across the vast, barren expanse of the New Jersey meadowlands, headed toward Cleveland. In her pocketbook—it had belonged to her mother—was almost two hundred dollars. She had taken that from a coffee can her father kept hidden in his workshop.

She also had taken three rings that belonged to her mother, and a watch that had belonged to her father's mother. She was set, she knew, for quite a while.

But, no matter what, she knew she could never go back.

And she got a good feeling when she pictured her father's face when he discovered his money and the jewelry were missing. He would yell and scream like he always did, but there was nothing he could do about it. She would not be around to beat.

Bobby Jo looked out the window, through the pale reflected image of her face. She wished that Steve were with her. Maybe she would call him when she reached Cleveland.

But what could she say to him? She shuddered at the idea of telling him the truth, at least all the truth. She couldn't bear that.

She put her hand into the shopping bag and felt Sport.

She glanced to her left. Sitting there was an old lady who had gotten on the bus with her in New York. Her eyes were closed, and she appeared to be sleeping.

Slowly, and softly, Bobby Jo moved her leg until it was touching the old woman's leg.

After a while, she fell asleep.

CHAPTER 6

At one o'clock on the day the body was discovered, Benton met in the Five Three squad room with eight other detectives Lawless had assembled from the Five Three and three other precincts.

Benton detailed to them what he knew about lustmurderers, and his feeling about what had gone on thus far.

First, the killer had carefully selected the street on which the body was dumped. He might be a native of the Bronx, or simply someone who had researched the area thoroughly. The street was simply too good a location to have been picked randomly.

The girl had been killed within four hours of her body being discovered; its condition clearly showed that. Just how she was done was undetermined; the ME would soon have something on that.

The killer they were up against was clever, probably knew police procedure to some degree, and was likely Caucasian and in his twenties. This was all based on a lustmurderer profile, and in Benton's opinion it was probably true.

The killer would kill again—that was for sure. He couldn't control himself. In a very real way, the detectives were working against the clock.

"I don't mean to be dramatic," Benton said, "but there's somebody walking around right now who will die if this guy is not collared."

One of the detectives asked Benton a question that hadn't been raised before. "This guy is dangerous to females. How about cops. Would he go after us?"

"I don't know of any instance where a lustmurderer targeted a cop for killing," Benton answered, "but you have to assume armed and very dangerous."

Benton gave them a story to illustrate. "When Will King, a really clever, determined detective, tracked Albert Fish down, he relaxed his guard, because what he encountered when he made the collar was an old man sitting on a bed and weeping. So he didn't cuff him. And out in the hallway Albert suddenly turned and he was a tiger, a straight razor in each hand."

Benton also warned them that the killer might either reappear on the site or try to insinuate himself into the investigation.

One of the detectives suggested, humorously, that if a guy came into the watering hole with a bloody ax and asked about the case, they would probably be suspicious.

Benton emphasized the point. "These guys can be very clever. There was a writer named Ann Rule—an experienced writer of crime stories—who knew Ted Bundy for years before he was collared; in fact, when he was first suspected she dismissed it. Reason? She knew Ted couldn't be a bad guy."

The detectives decided to meet every other day, and do

fives—reports—daily. These would be given to Benton, who would serve as a clearinghouse for all information.

Specific assignments were given. Barbara Babalino was to try to make the victim. Lawless would check BCI for any similars. Benton would contact the FBI, and he and the other detectives would canvass buildings on Snake Hill.

It was suggested that this not be done at hours inconvenient to the inhabitants, when some cops would do it. Reason: That would almost guarantee a lack of cooperation.

Lawless was also able to get some people to stake out St. Bonaventure in case the killer came back.

The meeting broke up at around two-thirty. Benton immediately called Jim Brosnan at the FBI Behavioral Sciences Unit in Quantico to see if he was around. He was often out of town—and was now—but was expected to return in a day or two.

Onairuts did the post at three o'clock. Benton was there, feeling his usual mild revulsion despite having seen hundreds of autopsies.

Some things were confirmed, and some new information uncovered.

The killer had excised both the mons veneris and the vulva, leaving a "triangular defect" measuring six by seven by seven inches that exposed the victim's pubic symphysis.

It was Onairuts's opinion, as he had stated at the scene, that the person who did the cutting was skilled but not professionally trained.

Decapitation had been done through the "lower portion of the fourth cervical vertebral body." The cut mark was clean, indicating that some sort of chopping weapon had been employed.

There was minimal hemorrhage at the sites of decapitation, vulvectomy, and mastectomy, just another indication that the murder was committed elsewhere and the body dumped.

Semen was discovered on the inside of the left thigh. Swabs were taken from the defect and the anus for lab examination. There was no way to determine if the sperm was ejaculated before or after death. After was more likely.

Benton was most interested in the bites, or "tool marks," as forensic odontologists put it. In his mind, the distinction between what odontologists characterized as "sexually sadistic" and "ego cannibalistic" could sometimes be blurred. Not this time. These marks were clearly ego cannibalistic. Not only were there the teeth marks, but there was bruising: the flesh had been gripped by the teeth and pulled at the same time it was sucked. The person who inflicted the wounds was trying to absorb the life essences of the victim at the same time as he destroyed her. In a way, too, it was as if the killer had left part of himself on the victim. Again this suggested to Benton the question: Why? Why would one human being do this to another?

Onairuts confirmed the time of death: the victim had died within four hours of the time she had been found.

The most important piece of information was Onairuts's theory of the cause of death: asphyxia. He had found numerous petechial hemorrhages in the lining of the lungs consistent with strangulation, either manual or by ligature.

Onairuts told Benton that he would have the lab results of the autopsy by the next day.

As he left the morgue Benton passed what was popularly known as the "brain barrel." It was in here that the brains of autopsied victims were put in net bags and soaked in formaldehyde until they became, as an ancient ME once put it, the "consistency of Velveeta cheese," suitable for slicing slide samples off for examination.

Benton had loved finding out about the brain barrel. It was just the kind of gruesome and gory thing he grooved on.

But now, as he passed it, he became aware that this young woman's brain should have been going in there, and he thought of what Onairuts had said, that she had been in very good general health, and something started to well up in him. Anger. It was an emotion he tried to keep buried as best he could. It interfered with a homicide investigation. Plus it was a punishing kind of emotion—and the most destructive physically.

But there was something deeper. When he was young he got a distinct message from his mother and father. Anger was not appropriate, and would be punished. He became scared to express it.

But now he felt it. No matter how sympathetically he considered why a killer killed, or what made a lustmurderer a lustmurderer, the fact was that the killer had chopped down a young woman who probably had everything to live for. Her brain doesn't end up in a barrel; but her body is in a refrigerated box. Her life is over. She lies on the gurney, like a piece of garbage.

And this fuck, whatever formed him, walks the streets.

I will get you, Benton thought, *whatever you are. You cannot and will not be allowed to get away with this.*

Home in his apartment, he realized that he hadn't eaten. He made a lettuce and tomato sandwich on diet wheat bread and got out a can of diet soda. If he was going to die, he figured, he wasn't going to do it to himself.

He remembered what his doctor had said during his

physical the year before: "Your triglycerides and choles-terol are at concentration-camp levels." The statement had made Benton feel good—temporarily, of course.

Then he went to bed. He hadn't really slept in over twenty-four hours, and from experience he knew that it didn't pay to try to do any investigation without sleep—you miss things that can make the difference. Anyway, what he was planning to do had to wait for darkness. He set the alarm for eleven.

CHAPTER 7

The alarm pulled Benton out of a dreamless sleep.

He showered and shaved with his holstered .38 wadcutter hanging behind the locked door in case, ho-ho, Norman Bates tried to get into the bathroom while he was showering. He referred to the gun by the term used for its ammunition—bullets that could stop an irate, charging water buffalo.

Out of the shower he donned underwear, pants, and soft body armor. Most cops in uniform wore bulletproof vests. Benton figured he was one of the few—maybe the only one—who wore it most of the time. "You can never tell when someone's going to try to put a hurt on you," he'd say.

Though other cops would argue it was overkill, Benton even thought it inadequate. It could stop ordinary bullets and knife thrusts, but if someone shot him with Teflon-coated ammunition it would be no protection at all.

"Yeah," Piccolo had said. "It won't stop fucking mortar fire either."

He also strapped on an ankle gun.

Sometimes Benton wished he were partial to checked jackets, plain pants, and black shoes. He would have that certain look that perps could instantly spot as cop. Then no one would try to rip him off when he was in dangerous areas, as he was going to be. But he had a compulsion to dress in what could fairly be described as a princely fashion. It came from his youth. His mother and father always demanded that he dress like a prince, so he did. It was one of the few things he could ever remember their complimenting him about.

Then again, it was an area they were interested in.

He left the house about eleven-thirty and caught a cab on Pelham Parkway. When he told the driver he wanted to go to 178th and Webster, the old guy balked.

"Hey, mister," he said in a heavy Yiddish accent. "Vat years I got left I'd like to have left after tonight. So I can't drive you to 178th and Webster."

Benton was forced to show him his shield and tell him it was police business, but he felt guilty about it. He contemplated taking a 5-milligram Valium, but he didn't. Instead, he concentrated on the lovely Webster Avenue scenery rolling by. It occurred to him that the way to get rich in Fort Siberia was to have the franchise on corrugated metal doors.

The trip might not yield much, but he had to see. It was one thing to do a scene at a random time, and another during the period when the crime occurred. You couldn't imagine everything; as much as possible, you had to duplicate the actual scenario.

In this case, that meant coming at midnight.

Of course there was always the chance he'd run into the killer. Then he could collar him.

Could he? Probably. He was carrying two guns. But in all the seventeen years he had been on the job, only once did he have a violent confrontation, and then his life had been saved.

Terry Franconi. What a piece of work was she. Eighty years old and she had set herself up as bait for a push-in artist who, ultimately, might have killed Benton if it hadn't been for her actions—namely, hitting the perp on the head with a lamp while he was in the process of strangling Benton.

He had really only known her six months, and then one night she had passed away quietly in her sleep.

Benton remembered a lot of things about her, but mostly how calm she was.

He had visited her six or seven times after the case ended. She would offer him something to drink and a little goody like a piece of cake—fuck the cholesterol—and she would be more interested in him than herself. And once, on the next-to-last time he had seen her, he had asked what her secret of happiness was.

"I am happy," she said, "because I live in the present. I guess I'm one of those people who understand that the past is past, and that the future isn't here. All we have, George, is today."

He had wondered about her attitude toward death, but he didn't think it an appropriate question. She had volunteered some answers.

"I don't think about death. I think about life and love and my children and grandchildren, and anyway, when I do think about it I think it will mean that someday I will see my Arthur again. Before God took him home he said he would be seeing me again, and I believe that."

Benton had a thought. He wondered what he would

have turned out like if he had been raised by Arthur and Terry Franconi, instead of his own mother and father. He never really got the feeling he was loved by them. They took care of him, but they never loved him, or at least they never showed it.

He had left for college when he was seventeen. They had a little party for him, and his mother kissed him and his father shook his hand—his father never kissed anybody.

Kisses. How many times had his mother kissed him in his life? Twenty times?

That's why he had liked Joyce so much. He found it vaguely embarrassing, but he used to love it when she would go into what he called a kissing frenzy. He did have trouble returning the affection.

He saw a street sign and refocused. He shouldn't be thinking about this stuff now.

The cab pulled to a stop at 178th Street and Webster. Benton paid the driver, who burned rubber leaving. He watched him go. Down the block a black man hailed the cab, which, of course, didn't stop, but almost ran him down.

Benton looked north, then south along Webster. South there was a man two blocks away walking what looked like a pair of pit bull terriers. North there was a couple walking the other way. And there was very little traffic.

It was cold enough to condense his breath. That was good. Just like last night.

Benton watched the line of traffic lights stretching down Webster into the distance change from green to yellow to red and back to green again. Then he turned and looked up Snake Hill.

The city, obviously, wasn't wasting money on light bulbs. There was not a single street lamp lit. It looked more like a road leading up a mountain than a Bronx street.

Benton thought of Bundy and Gein and Heirens and Kemper and all the rest. He was trying to think the way they would.

One of their kind had been here, right here, less than thirty hours ago.

Benton took a breath and started up, walking fairly fast. Besides doing his job, it was a good opportunity to give himself a cardiac stress test. After all, he had only auscultated his heart eighteen hours ago.

He used his flashlight to climb until he figured he was about halfway up the hill.

It was then that he spotted a man coming out of a building across the street. He had a sleek animal, and for just a fleeting moment Benton thought it was a puma. Christ, he could imagine it charging across the street. He would have to go combat stance and cut it down with the wadcutter. If he could.

But it wasn't a puma. It was one of those dogs that looked anorexic that he didn't know the name of.

He came to the same alleys that he had checked during daylight hours. Now they looked more sinister. Alleys in Fort Siberia always seemed darker than alleys somewhere else, even in daylight. Of course, Benton knew this was crazy, but that's the way it seemed.

As soon as he was a few steps inside each of the alleys, he drew his .38 and carried it loosely at his side. Better to be safe than sorry.

Four alleys and fifteen minutes later a sweaty Benton was near the top of Snake Hill. It had become apparent that this lustmurderer had really done his homework: you could probably dump a dead elephant here and not be seen. There were lights in some of the apartment windows, but they didn't reflect enough light to illuminate anything. He hadn't seen any people at the windows.

He came to the mouth of St. Bonaventure, where the buildings were silhouetted blackly against the night sky. He assumed that the stakeout was in place; it was nice to know a couple of other cops were nearby.

A thought: Maybe he should have had a couple of cops watch the morgue. But how could the killer get a line on that? Easy, really. That would be the place, he would know, where all homicide victims in New York City were shipped.

Then again, Benton thought, just how would you cover it? Who would you look for? Lustmurderers were disguised as people.

Benton turned into St. Bonaventure and almost missed it.

It was a bag of some sort, on the sidewalk, close to the corner of the building on his right.

Benton flashed the light on it. It was a medium-size brown bag, the top folded down.

He tensed. The bag had not been there when he had made his earlier search. He tensed more. The bag was out of context. It didn't belong on a deserted street in Fort Siberia.

He used the end of the flashlight to carefully lift the folded flap, then opened the bag. He shone the light in.

The lustmurderer had been back. It was a piece of flesh.

What was it . . . ?

"Jesus Christ," Benton said out loud.

Within the bloody mass the end of a tampon peeked out.

CHAPTER 8

Benton's rage shattered his fear of expressing anger.

He trotted down St. Bonaventure holding his shield up. "Where are you?" he yelled.

Ten seconds later two cops, both young, one tall and one short, emerged from one of the buildings on the left side of the street about halfway down.

Benton led them to the bag. Neither said anything when he showed it to them and explained. But they looked green.

"The question is, how did the killer set this bag here without being seen?"

Both of the cops shook their heads.

"No one came down this block, either on foot or by vehicle," the tall cop said.

"No one," the shorter cop added.

"How long you been here?"

"The loo"—the taller one said, using the slang name for lieutenant—"put us out here at three. We were due for relief."

"You were in that building all day?"

"Yeah," the tall cop said, "and night."

Benton walked back down St. Bonaventure toward Snake Hill. The cops followed without knowing where he was going. He went down Snake Hill a few steps, then turned. He looked at the bag, then backed up until its view was blocked by the corner of a building. Almost stealthily, he approached the corner of the building, then squatted down and reached around the corner to touch the bag.

The killer could have placed the bag and no one on Snake Hill would have seen him—because the buildings were abandoned. The cops on St. Bonaventure could not have seen him either.

Benton felt the anger draining.

"You figure that's how he did it?" the shorter cop asked.

Benton nodded.

"Which means," the shorter cop said, "that he knew someone would be watching the street."

"Yeah," Benton said. "That's right."

Benton knew a lustmurderer could do this. But he had never directly experienced it. It took tremendous arrogance. It was a big risk.

What exactly he got out of it, Benton thought, was another question. But he—and other serial killers—certainly liked to walk the wire. Preferably if it was greased.

For a moment, Benton's mind switched to Ted Bundy. After Bundy attacked the girls at the Florida State sorority house, and with an army of police searching the scene, he attacked another girl less than a mile away—and was almost collared.

And Kemper. In an interview he described how he used to walk around with victims' heads in a photo bag.

61

And John Wayne Gacy. He held barbecues at his house while guests wondered what the sickening smell coming from the crawl space was.

And Ed Gein. He used the skin of victims to make lampshades, bones to make furniture, all out in the open. When you sat down in one of his armchairs it was just that.

A thought: In a way, he did the same thing himself. He liked to play dangerous games. Off and on for years he used to shoplift useless little trinkets that he would then discard.

Or slip into the subway without paying.

A couple of times he walked out of a restaurant without paying.

And more than once—many times—he had done these things while on the job, which would have gotten him in deep trouble if he got caught.

Why?

He didn't know, but he was struck by the similarity of the actions.

The two cops made the squeal from the radio they had in the building, and a half hour later two guys from CSU showed up.

Photos were taken of the bag, and the area was checked for further evidence. Then the bag was lifted with tongs into another bag. The crime scene unit would check for prints and other evidence, then they would send the part over to the morgue for lab tests. All of this would happen in the morning.

The two stakeout cops wondered if it was worthwhile going back into the building.

"He wouldn't show up again, would he?" the tall one asked Benton.

"We better not take a chance."

The cops went back to the stakeout, and Benton walked down Snake Hill.

No cabs came along, but a northbound bus stopped for him. The driver looked Korean. Benton thought he probably needed a fourth-degree black belt to travel this route.

He was able to get a gypsy cab at Fordham Road, which he had drop him in front of the garage where his car was parked.

He wasn't tired, and anyway he knew he had one thing to do before he went home.

He took the West Side Highway downtown, then got onto the FDR Drive. It was flanked on one side by parks, projects, and various commercial buildings and on the other by the East River.

Lights twinkled on the water from buildings lining the shore on the Queens side.

He remembered it. It must have been ten years earlier, a trip along the West Side Highway with Joyce at his side. They had been to a police benefit and she was sitting close to him; in those days she always sat close to him.

And then, another image, same highway, different car, same girl: They drove along, the same lights twinkling on the river, but years had passed, and now she sat close to the door, the radio on, filling the void between them.

There was only a little pang of loss now. He was on the track of a serial killer, a lustmurderer.

Thank God. He knew that beneath the work there was darkness. The work kept him sane.

A memory: of Elizabeth Short. She was the first case he had ever been interested in. They called it the Black Dahlia Case. It was never solved, but to this day it remained fascinating.

It, too, must have been the work of a lustmurderer. Benton had actually gone down to the publisher of the detective magazine where he had first seen the pictures and asked, straight out, if he could see the pictures of the Black Dahlia without the black bands across her. In other words, could he see the gore?

Benton smiled. He remembered. The editor he spoke with was a big jowly guy who smoked a cigar that gave off an aroma that was close to human feces.

Benton remembered his teeth, too, when he smiled. They were brown.

"Hey, kid, you got balls. You want to see the human crossword, you got it."

He was fourteen when he looked at those pictures, and they were the most shocking thing he had ever seen in his life. They set off an explosion of fear and fascination, and he kept looking for what seemed like forever. To this day, he could still recall the pictures of Elizabeth Short in five separate pieces lying on a garbage-strewn field in Los Angeles in January of 1946.

Black Dahlia. It was a case that would probably never be solved. But he would never forget it, because it was then that he discovered his fascination with the gross and the morbid. With murder. And the satisfaction.

Lustmurderers, the experts said, were fascinated with murder very early in life. First came fantasy—fantasizing about murder. They would fantasize for years. And then, finally, came the real thing. And it would set off a blood lust never to be quenched.

A lot of them had become interested in and then obsessed with detective magazines: the ones that showed women bound and dominated, raped and killed. In fact, Benton was aware of one scholarly paper on the subject where it was postulated that killers used detective magazines as aids to fantasizing about "sex" crimes and as a manual for how the police operated.

Benton had no doubt it was true.

He was interested in those magazines himself. He used to fantasize some of the same things lustmurderers fantasized: women bound up, raped, dominated, controlled.

But that was where it stayed with him. In his relationships with Joyce and a few other women, he never got into bondage or pain or any of that stuff. He could fantasize about raping a woman, but the real thing was revolting.

Why did he think about rape? Lustmurderers didn't normally rape. They were necrophiles, or nothing.

But some serial killers who weren't lustmurderers were also necrophiles. They liked the control too. Of course they had it all worked out.

He thought of a line, a classic from Henry Lee Lucas, who was asked why he would only have intercourse with a woman who was dead.

"I like peace and quiet," he said.

Still, Benton thought that understanding why a man raped someone would give him an answer as to why a lustmurderer murdered.

Somehow it was all bound up. And somehow, too, it might help explain why he was the way he was. That was really the only reason he was wondering at all, wasn't it?

For the moment, he could explain nothing.

Benton got off the FDR Drive at 23rd Street, looked around, and went uptown to 27th Street, where he parked opposite Bellevue, a huge complex of buildings that always seemed to be under construction.

Benton parked in a No Parking zone, the only space

available, flipped down the visor with an NYPD Official Business sign on it, and walked to the corner of 28th Street. When the light changed, he crossed the street.

He didn't really know who he was looking for, or what he looked like.

Images: handsome, smiling Ted Bundy, exuding boyish charm. Wayne Gacy, a heavyset man shaking hands with Rosalynn Carter, or Gacy dressed as a clown, entertaining at a children's center. Who could know that the smiling eyes within the clown face were the eyes of a serial murderer?

Still, it was possible to see something in a person's eyes, even if you weren't trained to look for it. In Florida there had been at least one girl in a disco who had seen something bad in Bundy's eyes and refused his offer to drive her home.

She said they looked "funny, scary."

It was a perception that had saved her life. Thirty minutes later he was in the sorority house a few blocks from the disco slaughtering people.

Benton looked at the people passing the hospital and going in and out of it: nurses, doctors, people with a concerned look on their faces probably visiting patients, cops. There seemed to be more cops at Bellevue than anywhere else in the city.

There were a surprising number of people around for such a late hour. Benton looked at people passing him by as he made his way to one side of the hospital where there was an entrance under construction.

Just before he went in, he heard the distant sound of an emergency ambulance. That was another thing that kept Bellevue busy.

Inside, the entrance opened onto a long lobby that led to

a reception area. To go beyond this, you had to get past uniformed private security guards.

He stood watching traffic at the desk, particularly young white males. There weren't many.

He also watched anyone going up to a guard to speak. There were many restricted areas beyond the guards, but one in particular that a lustmurderer might be interested in: the morgue. Might he not think, Benton thought as he watched, something like "I put you there, bitch. Just dropped by to say hello." It was not, Benton figured, beyond the pale of reason, but it was a very thin chance.

Nevertheless something in Benton told him to stay—and watch.

He stayed three hours, by the end of which time, he knew, the guards were watching him. He left just as dawn was coming up. He had guessed wrong, or he had just missed the look—or maybe the look wasn't there. He'd have to hope for another chance.

CHAPTER 9

Benton stopped at Papa John's and treated himself to a full breakfast—two eggs every two weeks was not excessive—and was in the squad room by seven o'clock.

Lab test results were in on the girl, and CSU had dropped off the photos.

There was nothing extraordinary about the test results.

She was not on any controlled substances of any sort, and she had eaten within six hours of her death. The substance on her thigh was confirmed as semen, but none was found in the defect. No doubt, Benton thought, they would find evidence of semen in the vulva, though. There was no evidence of semen in the anus, or what was left of it.

There were ninety-two 8 × 10 color photographs of the body at the scene and at the morgue, taken from every conceivable angle, both long shots and close-ups.

He went through them twice, lingering each time at the photos that clearly showed the position the killer had placed her in.

And "placed" was the word. Random dumping could not have left her as she was. A fetal position. The killer had arranged her to look like a baby.

It could almost be seen as a kindly, caring act, an act of tenderness.

Almost.

Benton didn't know what it meant, though he sensed that it had a very specific meaning that, somehow, he should be able to understand. He stared at the pictures a long time, shuffling and reshuffling them, but with no luck.

At eight o'clock, Benton met in the squad room with the other detectives working the case. He began by telling them of the discovery of the organ at the crime scene, but he said that he was not hopeful that anything useful would come out of the tests being run on it. The perp would have made sure of that.

"That means," Benton said, "that the killer placed it there sometime between around three o'clock in the afternoon and the time I got there."

"In daylight?" a beefy detective named Galligan asked.

"Maybe," Benton said. He looked through the haze of smoke that was collecting in the room. He had a hope. Five cops were canvassing the buildings during the day and into the early evening hours. Maybe one had spotted the killer without realizing it.

"Does anyone recall anyone carrying a bag in the area? I mean any size bag?"

There was no response from the group for a while. Then Galligan spoke. "I saw a couple of ladies carrying shopping bags."

Frank Piccolo added, "I seen a UPS truck. Guy made a

delivery, but that wasn't anywhere near St. Bonaventure. It was the middle of the block."

"Will you check that out, Frank?" Benton said.

"What?"

"Whether in fact a delivery was made. These guys will try anything."

There was a little silence. Then a hand went up in the back of the room. It was a thin young cop who Benton knew had just been sent over to Siberia from the Four Six. He looked troubled.

"I might have seen something," he said. "It was about four o'clock. I was way down the block, so I couldn't see too well. But it was a young guy. I wasn't close enough to make him, but from the way he walked you could tell he was young. He was carrying something—an overnight bag."

The cop paused. It looked like his face was blotchy. This wasn't easy.

"I know this because I stopped to watch him. I wondered if he was going to go into St. Bonaventure. He didn't. He went into the building on the corner, so I stopped watching him."

Benton waited a moment.

The cop said, "But I discovered later that that building was empty."

"Why later?"

"I didn't know it was empty at the time. Something about the situation just didn't sit right, which is why I checked it out. But I didn't see the bag around the corner."

"He probably went into the building," Benton said, "because he knew you were watching him."

The cop nodded. From his expression Benton could tell that's what he had figured too.

"This guy's balls," Piccolo said, "go clang."

"What'd he look like?" Benton asked.

"He looked pretty big. Not fat. Big. And he had light hair."

"What about a vehicle? Anybody see anything at all unusual, now that you think about it?"

There were no answers.

"Okay," Benton said. "I'd like everyone to get their fives done before leaving. I assume no one has anything else worth reporting to the group?"

There was no response. Benton looked at Lawless, who was off to his right leaning against a desk.

Lawless turned toward the detectives. "I haven't come up with anything at BCI yet."

"We haven't gotten an ID yet," Barbara said, "but a couple of leads are being worked on."

"It's a miracle," Benton said, "but so far the media haven't grabbed this. That is bound to change, of course. The case is stirring some interest downtown, but so far no one has volunteered to help us canvass."

There was laughter. In most cases police brass were political animals interested in only one thing: keeping their asses intact. The idea of captains or deputy inspectors knocking on apartment doors in Fort Siberia was a laughable one to street cops.

The meeting broke up with another tentatively set for two days later. Meetings could be fruitful, but Benton and Lawless didn't believe in calling them willy-nilly.

At around ten-thirty Benton put another call through to Jim Brosnan at the BSU.

Brosnan was still not in. The woman who answered the

phone said that she'd have him call Benton back, but that wouldn't be until at least the next day.

Benton could imagine where Brosnan was: sticking his nose into one serial murder or another. Over the last few years, he had told Benton on his last foray to Washington, serial murders had risen dramatically. An astonishing 80 percent of all murders were done by repeat offenders.

"You collar one," Brosnan had said to Benton, "and your stats drop significantly."

Five minutes after calling Brosnan, Benton headed for the crime scene. He would do some of the canvassing himself, then return to the station house sometime in the afternoon for paperwork. By then, he hoped, the rest of the forensics would be in and the ME would have a report on the vulva.

CHAPTER 10

Barbara Babalino had gotten two missing-person reports from Sam Turner, the desk sergeant. One had been phoned in on the morning of November 3, the day the body was discovered. The other had been phoned in a few hours later.

Both described missing white females, one named Carol Schultheis, twenty-two, who lived off Fordham Road in the Bronx and worked in a deli, and the other Michelle Reynolds, twenty-one, an X-ray technician at Jacobi Hospital.

It was very unusual, Barbara thought, for there to be two missing people in one precinct over such a short period of time. She hoped they weren't related.

They weren't. Carol Schultheis turned up even before Barbara began to check her out. Apparently she had gotten drunk—an unusual event for her—and had stayed at a friend's house.

By the afternoon of November 3, Barbara had not yet had time to check out the second girl. Turner told her that he had gotten a call from a rather distraught mother, Linda Reynolds. Mrs. Reynolds said on weekdays she usually saw her daughter only for a brief period in the morning because she worked nights and her daughter days, but when she had awakened that morning her daughter wasn't there—and her bed hadn't been slept in.

The woman told Turner her daughter was not the type to fool around. She and Michelle were very close because her husband was dead, and they always liked to tell each other where they were.

Linda Reynolds had called Jacobi Hospital, where Michelle worked as a radiologist, and she had been told that Michelle had not reported for her shift.

Mrs. Reynolds was very scared. She described her daughter as being very pretty, about five five, with blond hair and brown eyes. She had never done anything like this. They cared about each other's feelings too much.

Turner could have asked her a number of questions, but he didn't. The woman was close to tears, and Turner sensed that there might be something to it.

The woman lived off Pelham Bay Parkway, not far from the hospital. Barbara called her, and she picked up before the first ring was complete. She sounded very disappointed when Barbara identified herself. Barbara asked if she could come over and take some information. Mrs. Reynolds said she would appreciate that very much.

The apartment building, on Williamsbridge Road, was in a primarily Italian neighborhood that was safe, for the same reason that Pleasant Avenue, in the heart of Harlem, and the Arthur Avenue area, in the center of Bronx decay, were safe: La Cosa Nostra lived there, and "if you did the crime, don't worry about doin' the time," as one cop put it, "because there won't be no time."

74

Barbara rang the bell and was immediately buzzed in. She felt torn. On the one hand she wanted this to be the girl so they could have the positive ID; on the other, she did not want it to be anybody.

The woman who opened the door to the Reynolds apartment was a small blond woman who looked to be about fifty. She seemed relieved—and unnerved—by Barbara's announcing who she was.

The woman led her into the living room. It was typically Bronx, or Queens, or Brooklyn. Barbara had seen a thousand middle-class living rooms just like it.

They sat down, Mrs. Reynolds in an armchair, Barbara sitting on a couch opposite her. The woman's eyes were red. She blinked constantly, and her hands were always moving.

Barbara tried to disregard it. She had to keep her own head clear. An image from St. Bonaventure Street intruded, but she fought it away.

As delicately as possible, Barbara asked Mrs. Reynolds about her daughter.

At first, the woman was hesitant; it was as if she feared that if she talked about her daughter as possibly missing, she would never come back. But at Barbara's gentle urging she talked. She told Barbara about her daughter's shifts—she worked only days—and about her dedication—how she would smile at patients she knew were very ill and then come home and cry about it. That she was a good girl who did not have time for a boyfriend right now, and who had never given Mrs. Reynolds any trouble at all.

Barbara asked her nonchalantly if she had any pictures of her daughter. Mrs. Reynolds had about five thousand, she said.

She brought out four albums and set them on a coffee

table by the couch, then leafed through them. She asked what Barbara was interested in.

It was hard to tell from the pictures whether the girl shown was the same as on the street. But one thing was for sure: Mrs. Reynolds had not lied about her daughter's looks. She was a pretty blonde with brown eyes and a very nice figure. A figure, Barbara thought, not unlike her own.

Barbara asked if she could take a couple of the pictures, and Mrs. Reynolds readily agreed.

At the door, Mrs. Reynolds said, "Do you think you'll find her soon?"

"Yes," Barbara said, and thought that, one way or another, they would

From Mrs. Reynolds's house Barbara drove to Jacobi Medical Center on Pelham Bay Parkway, which was actually close enough for her to walk.

She went to personnel, then was directed to the security division. Fortunately, an ex-cop was director and Barbara was able to get a copy of Michelle Reynolds's prints without any hassle whatsoever. Twenty minutes later she was handing the prints to a clerk in BCI. It wouldn't be long before they would know if the girl on St. Bonaventure Street was the girl in the pictures.

Barbara's thinking had clarified: she hoped it wasn't.

CHAPTER 11

Benton returned to the Five Three squad room after four hours of canvassing the buildings on Snake Hill. As he had expected, cooperation was almost nil. Half of the people didn't even speak English.

He found an envelope Barbara Babalino had left him. In it was a note that told him of her visit to Mrs. Reynolds and that there was a possibility the Reynolds girl was the victim. She said she had not questioned Mrs. Reynolds extensively.

She also told him that she had obtained Michelle Reynolds's prints and sent them through BCI to see if they could get a match.

She left three 4 × 5 color pictures of the missing girl.

One showed her in a bathing suit campily posing at the beach, another was a close-up portrait shot, and the third showed her in her white uniform, with three other girls.

Benton knew the background in the picture: Jacobi Hospital. He had taken Beth over there once to get her stomach pumped when she had ingested a bottle of baby aspirin, and he had taken himself over there three times, once when he secretly suspected a stroke—it turned out he had an ear infection—and twice when he thought he was having a coronary. The first attack turned out to be Joyce's chili; the second was Vita Herring.

The girl was beautiful, and from her smile Benton sensed an inner happiness.

He looked again at the picture of her in a bathing suit. Prurient interest mixed with professional—and something else: fear. He could not prove it, he could not tell you why, but the lines of Michelle Reynolds's body followed the same lines, however disfigured, of the girl on St. Bonaventure Street.

He filed the materials away and made himself a cup of instant Sanka. He would never drink the brewed coffee that was almost always available, and not only because of the caffeine content.

No. It was because Maurice Gang, the detective who usually made it, had a theory that coffee was better in a pot that was not cleaned out. "It adds richness and bouquet," he would argue.

Some detectives, Benton included, would argue that it added the ability to strip furniture.

He was halfway through the Sanka, sitting at a desk poring over a five, when the phone rang. He picked up and listened for a moment, then hung up. He put the coffee down. He knew he wouldn't finish it.

The body had a name: Michelle Reynolds.

CHAPTER 12

Benton immediately left the station house and drove over to Snake Hill. If possible, he wanted to find Barbara so she could join him in following through with the victim's mother.

He drove up and down Snake Hill twice but couldn't see her; in fact he didn't see a single detective. Perhaps, he thought, they had all been killed.

He left the scene. Speed was essential. There was always the possibility that Mrs. Reynolds would find out that her daughter was dead, and then he could lose her potential value as a source of information. She would be gone to grief.

Benton called the Reynolds house from a pay phone on Webster. Mrs. Reynolds answered. He identified himself and told her that there was some additional information he wanted to get. She agreed to see him right away.

Ten minutes later, Benton was in the living room, sitting on the same couch Barbara had sat on, a pen poised over a notebook. Mrs. Reynolds sat in an armchair opposite him.

"Like I said," Benton said, "I just want to get a few more details."

"I think it's great the way the police help people. People are wrong when they say the police don't care."

Benton looked blankly at her.

"So," he said, "when do you usually see Michelle?"

"I'm a waitress at Hugo's Cafeteria downtown. You know that place? I work nights. Start at four and get home late, so I usually just see her before she goes to work early in the morning. She starts at eight. But we always try to have breakfast together."

Suddenly, Mrs. Reynolds started to cry.

Benton felt a surge of guilt.

"Try to relax," he said when the sobbing had subsided to some degree.

"Do you think Michelle will come back?"

"Sure," Benton said. *Christ.*

Mrs. Reynolds nodded, regained her composure.

"When is the last time you saw her?"

"The day before yesterday. I saw her in the morning. We had breakfast together." Mrs. Reynolds seemed on the verge of crying again.

"How does she go to work?" Benton asked.

"She drives."

"She never stays out late, or stays over, right?"

"That's right. She only stayed out late a couple of times, but she always told me."

"Does she have a boyfriend?"

"She could easily. But she's too busy at the hospital."

"What kind of car does she have?"

"1979 LTD."

"What color?"

"The top is brown, like a tan, the bottom dark blue."

"She parks at the hospital?"

"Yes. She has a spot in back. I checked. The car's not there. It's also not where she parks it down here, right off Ogden."

"I assume you've checked with all her friends about her whereabouts."

Mrs. Reynolds nodded.

"Can you give me their names and numbers anyway?"

Mrs. Reynolds went out of the room for a moment, then came back with a small address book. She gave Benton the names of five women and their numbers.

When she was finished, Benton asked, "Do you know, Mrs. Reynolds, if your daughter was worried about anything. Did she have anything on her mind that was unusual?"

"No. She would have told me."

Benton nodded and was about to speak when the woman spoke again, abruptly.

"I . . . I do remember a . . . a while ago—two weeks ago?—she said something odd to me."

Benton looked at her.

"She said she got a sort of creepy feeling that she was being watched. Somebody was watching her."

"Where?"

"She wasn't sure. At work she felt it, and sometimes while she was driving."

"She didn't say who?"

"No."

"She said nothing else about it?"

"No. It was just a feeling she had."

Mrs. Reynolds, who had been watching Benton carefully, brightened. "You don't think it means anything, do you?"

Benton shook his head no. He flipped his notebook closed. "That's all I have," he said, standing up.

Mrs. Reynolds stood up. She followed Benton as he drifted toward the front door.

"I'm going to stay home," the woman said, "until Michelle is found. You can reach me here. Anytime. Okay?"

"Thank you," he said, and was gone.

On the street, he found a phone booth and tried the first number on the list Mrs. Reynolds had given him. No answer.

A woman named Sue Homan answered at the second number. Benton identified himself, then asked her if Michelle had ever mentioned to her that she felt she was being watched. The answer was negative.

He then asked a number of questions in order to learn that the Reynolds girl went to St. Martin's Church on Pelham Parkway.

Benton thanked Sue Homan and hung up.

He called the other three women on the list. Two were out. One, by the name of Ivette Marcella, was in.

He told her he was investigating the case and wondered if Michelle had ever mentioned anyone watching her.

No, Michelle had never said anything like that.

Benton thanked Ivette Marcella and hung up, then stepped out of the booth.

He looked up and took a deep breath. The sky was powder blue, the cumulus clouds high and beautiful, the weather comfortably cool.

Oh yeah.

*   *   *

Benton drove over to St. Martin's Church, which was only a few blocks from Williamsbridge Road. He spoke to the pastor, a kindly-looking old guy named Quinn.

As it happened, Father Quinn knew Mrs. Reynolds. She had been very helpful once in a buffet the church had held.

Father Quinn volunteered to tell Mrs. Reynolds about her daughter.

Benton thanked him and left, feeling a little guilty that he didn't do it himself.

But not so guilty, he thought, that he would go back and offer his services. It was a short drive from the Reynolds apartment to Jacobi Hospital, a vast complex of cream-colored brick buildings on Pelham Bay Parkway. He parked on a side street, then entered via the main entrance.

The Radiology Department was on the second floor of the building; to get access Benton had to show his tin to one of the scruffy, mangy-haired Hispanic guards sealing off the elevators and stairs.

Benton's path was circuitous, taking him down about four separate hallways, the last one taking him past a lot of new construction. He paused to look through the window of a door. He could see a large room that contained a huge variety of electronic equipment. It was unfinished.

The chief of radiology's office, at one end of a short hall, was by comparison a rathole. The chief must have been chief for a while. The wood nameplate on the door, CHARLES MCKENNA, was faded. He tapped on the door, which was partially open, then pushed it open all the way.

The man sitting behind the desk looked up. He was young, with curly brown hair and gentle eyes: a kindly face.

Benton wondered if he was a killer.

"I'm George Benton," he said, taking out his shield. "I'm from the Fifty-third Precinct. I wonder if I could speak to you about Michelle Reynolds."

The man blinked. "Is she okay?"

"We're just looking into her disappearance."

"Please come in."

Benton went into the office.

The man stood up, reached across the desk, and offered his hand. Benton shook it.

"I'm Charles McKenna," he said. They sat down. Benton could smell fear coming off him.

"We're very concerned," he said. "This is very unusual for her. She's never late, and never misses a day. She has a very old-fashioned value system."

He paused. A soft wave of something, almost undetectable, passed across McKenna's face. Loss? Longing? Benton couldn't read it for sure.

"When was the last time you saw her?"

"Day before yesterday. Monday. She was working on a cat."

"At cat?"

McKenna almost smiled. "I'm sorry. A cat scan. I'm breaking her into that. I plan to make her head of that section."

Benton looked at him. He decided to get right to it.

"I spoke with her mother a while ago," he said, "and she indicated that Michelle had a feeling that someone was watching her here. Did she say anything to you?"

Benton thought a little blood drained out of McKenna's face.

"In fact she did. About two weeks ago. We were in the cafeteria having coffee. She said she got this creepy feeling someone was watching her."

"Who?"

"I asked her. She couldn't pinpoint it. I . . . until now I didn't think much of it. I mean, being an radiologist is a very stressful job. I mean, she's done as many as fifteen cats a shift."

Benton nodded. "She didn't say anything more? Nothing about who might be watching her?"

"Well she seemed to want to. She said . . . she felt it most when she was in open spaces, like the parking area, the cafeteria, when she was driving . . . uh . . . like that."

"I guess you have a lot of people around here, huh?" Benton asked.

"Sure. Patients in and out. It's been sort of a madhouse since the construction started." McKenna paused.

"Do you think she might have told this to anyone else here?" Benton asked.

McKenna blinked. "I don't know. I could ask."

"I'd appreciate that."

McKenna went out of the office; he returned a few minutes later with two women, both young and dressed in nurses' uniforms. They looked nervous.

Benton asked them the question, and they both said no.

McKenna turned to Benton. "The other technician is busy, but I asked her. She doesn't remember Michelle saying anything like that."

"Okay. Thanks." Benton could feel the disappointment lying in his belly. "Could you show me where Michelle parks?" he asked.

"Her car's not there," McKenna said.

"How do you know?"

"I checked. I checked as soon as her mother called."

"I'd just like to see the spot."

"Sure."

McKenna lead Benton through a maze of halls to an exit in the rear of the hospital.

There was a huge parking lot with one side parallel to Simpson Street and the other to the Pelham Bay Parkway, which was separated from it by a wrought-iron fence.

The lot was perhaps half-filled.

"She parks here," McKenna said, stopping at a spot perhaps fifty yards from the exit, "or at least in this area."

Benton scanned the area. "Thanks," he said.

"Please call me when you find out something."

Benton nodded.

Benton returned to the Five Three. Reports from the ME's office and Forensic were waiting for him.

The tests on the vulva were positive. High levels of acid phosphatase had been found inside it, and some living sperm. There was no determination on whether the vulva was in situ when the assault was perpetrated.

CSU, unfortunately, had nothing substantial. No trace of the killer, not a hair, not a single fiber, was found anywhere.

Benton figured that the reverse was true of the killer.

There were sixteen DD5 reports to read.

Benton read them carefully twice, but there was nothing in them. The populace was essentially as he thought it would be: not helpful.

Either people had noticed nothing out of the ordinary, or they wouldn't cooperate at all.

Piccolo and Edmunton had put out feelers to their informants, but so far nothing had come back. Benton doubted anything would.

Lawless came into the squad room at about four-thirty.

He saw Benton at the desk and came over to him. "How's it going, George?"

Benton told Lawless about the ID, and talking to the mother, and to McKenna, the chief technician. And about the feeling the young woman got that someone was watching her.

"The parking lot," he said, "would be a good spot for him to grab her. I'm going to check it out."

"Good. Unfortunately I won't be able to help anymore. We got some new business in a short while ago."

"What's that?"

"A couple of grounders down by 179th Street.

"I'll keep you posted," Benton said.

Benton arrived at the parking lot just as dark was descending, maybe, he thought, the time of day that Michelle Reynolds had walked to her car.

He pulled his BMW into one of the middle spaces facing the hospital, got out, and stood near the car.

Within thirty seconds, he could see three young women dressed in white uniforms coming out of the hospital toward the banks of cars. He went over to them as casually as possible.

"Hello," he said chirpily, reaching into his jacket pocket and pulling out his shield, "My name is George Benton and I'm a detective in the Fifty-third Precinct. I wonder if you could help me."

They were young, Hispanic. They tensed a bit, though they smiled.

"I was wondering if any of you came out about this time Monday night. What I'm really interested in is whether you might have seen a young blond-haired woman—maybe you know her—get into a car with anyone."

The smallest of the trio proved the boldest. "What's her name, man?"

"Michelle Reynolds."

They didn't react.

"Did you see anyone?"

Two of the women shook their heads. "No," said the smallest.

"Thanks," Benton said.

Over the next hour Benton questioned fifty people. Others got to their cars before he could question them. But he figured that he could and would come back every night of the week. Somebody must have seen something—assuming the snatch had occurred here.

Benton left about nine-thirty and drove back across Pelham Parkway toward his house. As he passed Williamsbridge Road he glanced down it.

Somewhere down there a mother is crying for her daughter. Life, he thought, *is so full of sadness.*

CHAPTER 13

At nine o'clock the next morning Benton was at one of the desks in the Five Three squad room poring over the reports from the previous day. The phone rang.

He picked up. "Detective Benton."

"Yes, Detective," said the faraway voice, which Benton recognized instantly, "do you know what the leading cause of death in Florida is now?"

"No."

"The electric chair."

Benton laughed. Most people thought of the FBI as a bunch of stuffed shirts. Some were. Most weren't—and certainly not Jim Brosnan.

"And did you know why the governor of Florida had to get himself a word processor?"

"No."

"He got writer's cramp signing death warrants."

Benton laughed again.

"How are you, Jim?"

"Well, you know, we miss the director. The chance to serve in Seattle, Nome, and those other nice places."

"Don't forget Broken Rifle, Colorado."

Brosnan laughed. "How you doin' George?"

"I'm okay. I need your help."

"Speak."

"It looks like we have a lustmurderer operating up here. I wanted to see if he's known to you guys."

"What's his MO?"

Benton gave the MO.

Brosnan's response was immediate. "That's Henry the Eighth. All his women lose their heads. He's been working the Northeast for about a year. We know him well."

"How many victims?"

"Ten."

"Make it eleven," Benton said. "Where's he operating?"

"Mostly Jersey—Lincroft, Parsippany, Freehold, Holmdel, but one on Staten Island. Now one in the Bronx."

"How far apart?"

"Well, one a month, starting in January."

"Any leads?"

"No. This guy's very cute. And getting better with the blade. You know, practice makes perfect."

It was not an idle statement. The more someone murdered, the better he became at it, better at doing it—and at covering his tracks. It was like mastering a trade.

"I'd like to come down and see what you've got," Benton said. "When can I do that?"

"Tomorrow morning?"

"Is that the best you can do, Jim?"

"How would you like to be audited for the last twenty-five years?"

Benton laughed.

"I'm in at eight," Brosnan said.

"Thanks, Jim. See you on the morrow."

"Looking forward to it, George."

Benton hung up and looked at the phone.

How terrible the event of murder, he thought, *and yet Jim and I joke and laugh. And life goes on.*

CHAPTER 14

Bobby Jo Johnson sat in the waiting room at Grand Central Station.

She had been in the city for two weeks: Cleveland had proved too cold. In fact, she had never been in a colder place in her life. She wondered how anyone could live there year-round—God! It wasn't even winter yet.

Four days earlier she had run out of money, even the money she had gotten from selling the watches and rings.

Now she was thinking about going home, and the thought depressed her. Her father would have her back, she felt. But first he would give her a beating, and then he would use her. They would be right back where they started from.

Plus, he would have the satisfaction of seeing her crawl back. She didn't want that, not for that bastard.

But she didn't have much choice. For two days she had slept in building hallways, and the last two on a bench in the station waiting room.

She had eaten by begging, stealing, and once, three days earlier, by eating a complete delicious meal at a restaurant and then walking out without paying.

Now she nibbled—though she wanted to inhale it—on a Milky Way bar she had stolen from one of the newsstands in the station.

She felt as alone as she ever had in her entire life, like when Mommy and Daddy got mad at her when she was little.

The place was so big, like a big cave, and the people passing by didn't care about her. In fact, she had a feeling they disliked her. A couple of times she got tears in her eyes thinking about it.

She had a hollow feeling in her stomach. She wondered where she would sleep tonight. She wouldn't stay in the station again. Twice men had bothered her. Once a filthy, smelly bum had poked her awake; he had spoken to her, but she had no idea what he was talking about.

Another time a well-dressed man with white hair had asked her if she was "sporting." She didn't know what he meant either, but she didn't want to go anywhere with him.

Bobby Jo took the last bite of the Milky Way and licked her fingers.

She would have to go back. Back to the house. If Daddy would have her.

Of course he would. But there were no guarantees. Maybe he wouldn't. Could that be? Her stomach rumbled.

Bobby Jo was sitting on the front bench, looking through a huge arch into the main concourse, where she would see part of the information kiosk—and people. She had never seen so many people in her life, except when she first went to Pennsylvania Station to take the bus to Cleveland. They hurried back and forth like they didn't know anyone else existed.

Distracted by the people in the main concourse Bobby Jo didn't notice him until he was standing in front of her. He was quite a sight.

He was a tall, thin colored guy, very well dressed in a suit and tie and white shirt. He had very nice features, and his hair seemed to be wavy rather than kinky. He had very large soft brown, almost black eyes.

"Could you tell me," he said, "where the Forty-fifth Street exit to this place is?"

He smiled. His teeth were very straight and white.

Bobby Jo, from all she had heard of her father talking about niggers, should have been afraid of this man, but she wasn't, not at all.

"No," she said. "I don't. I don't know where anything is. I'm not from here."

"Where you from?"

"The Bronx."

He nodded. "I have friends who live up there."

He sat down next to her. He smelled good. She hoped she didn't smell.

"I'm Earl," he said, putting out his hand. "Earl Watkins."

She hesitated a moment, then took his hand. It was very soft and warm.

"Bobby Jo," she said. "Bobby Jo Johnson."

Earl frowned. He looked very concerned. "May I say something?"

Bobby Jo blinked. "Yes."

"You okay? You look a little . . . uh . . . hungry, maybe."

Bobby Jo felt something surge inside her. She felt close to tears. She said nothing.

"Will you give me the pleasure," Earl said, "of buying you some breakfast?"

Bobby Jo hesitated only a moment, then she was walking out with him. He seemed to know exactly where he was going.

Even Bobby Jo didn't know how hungry she was. Earl took her to a pancake house not far from the station and she ate two orders of pancakes, smeared with butter and doused with syrup, and a half-dozen sausages and two large glasses of milk.

"That your problem, pretty little Bobby Jo," Earl said. "You hungry."

Bobby Jo smiled. She felt a little nervous with Earl, but she felt good too.

He offered her a cigarette from a pack of Chesterfields. Bobby Jo didn't smoke, but she wanted to please Earl. She took one, and he lit it with a gold lighter. She noticed that every single one of his fingers except the thumb had a ring on it. And all were polished.

"What beautiful rings," she said.

"They ain't nothing compared to your beauty, little Bobby Jo."

Bobby Jo felt her face flush. She got a good feeling deep inside her. She hadn't felt this good in a long time.

"You one of the prettiest childs I ever did see."

Bobby Jo bowed her head a little.

"I just call it like it is," Earl said. "You like more to eat?"

"No, I'm full. Thanks."

The waitress came over and topped off the coffee Earl was drinking. He added some sugar and milk, then took a sip. Then he put the cup down and looked evenly at Bobby Jo. "Where'd you stay last night?"

"In the station."

"You couldn'ta slept well, huh?"

"No." She felt herself filling up a little.

Earl reached inside his jacket; when he took his hand out he had in it the largest wad of cash Bobby Jo had ever seen. It was folded over and held together by a gold money clip in the shape of a dollar sign. He took the clip off, unfolded the money, and pulled off a fifty. He laid it in front of Bobby Jo.

"You take this," he said. "I don't think a young beautiful girl like you has to be sleeping in a railroad station."

"I can't take this."

"Sure you can. And you will."

"Thank you." Bobby Jo felt her eyes get misty.

Earl just kept looking at her, a little smile on his face. He took a drag on the cigarette, and the smoke trailed out of his nose, which was not like the noses of most colored people she had seen. He was really quite handsome.

Five minutes later they left the restaurant and walked along 43rd Street. As they walked, Bobby Jo became aware of passersby stealing a glance or simply looking in disgust at them. She didn't care. In fact, she liked the idea of walking with Earl.

They walked west across Manhattan to the river and watched the activity at the piers where the great ocean liners were docked. Then they started walking north.

Bobby Jo had no idea where they were going, and she didn't care. She just liked being with him, and after a while she felt very safe. He was easy to talk to, and it wasn't long before she told him that she had run away from home, and what her father was like, and her mother, and that there was nothing there for her. She didn't want to go back.

Of course she didn't tell him all the things her father did to her. She would have been too embarrassed.

She also didn't tell him that she was fourteen. She said she was seventeen, and he seemed to believe her.

Earl stopped walking when she'd finished telling him about her home life and told her she was too smart and pretty to have to take stuff like that. He said that maybe he could help her.

She asked him how, and he said he would tell her later; he wanted it to be sure.

At West End Avenue and 70th Street Earl stopped again. "You know," he said, "we ain't too far from where I live. Would you like to come up awhile?"

The idea was a little scary, but she felt compelled to go.

"Okay," she said.

"First, though, let's go in here."

The next thing she knew, Earl was ushering her through the door of a store on the corner. It sold ladies' things.

"All right," Earl said, "I want you to pick out a couple of nice dresses for yourself, and whatever else you need."

"Oh," Bobby Jo said. "Oh!"

Earl helped Bobby Jo pick out the dresses. They were more grown-up than anything Bobby Jo—or even her mother—had owned—very tight-fitting.

Bobby Jo felt a little funny walking around in them, but Earl encouraged her when he whispered, "Your figure is a gift from God, honey, and you honor him when you display it."

Bobby Jo was surprised by the dress shop—and surprised and impressed by where Earl lived. It was on 72nd

Street and West End Avenue and had a big canopy over the sidewalk and a uniformed doorman.

"How are you, Mr. Watkins?" the doorman said as she and Earl passed by him and entered the building.

They took the elevator to the eighth floor and walked down a carpeted hall to Earl's apartment.

He let her go in first. She stepped into the living room.

It was breathtaking, the biggest, most beautiful room she had ever seen in her life. The walls were bright pink, the ceiling white, the wall-to-wall carpeting a bright yellow, the furniture, which looked like it was made of leather, white. There were many paintings on the walls, but Bobby Jo couldn't tell what they were of, except one that looked like a guitar. Against the left wall was a bar with a floor-to-ceiling mirror that reflected the entire room and made it seem even bigger. Close to it, set on a pedestal, was an all-white statue of a horse that seemed only slightly smaller than life-size.

"It's beautiful," Bobby Jo said.

"I decorated it myself. Let me show you the rest of it."

Earl took Bobby Jo on a tour of the other five rooms of the apartment. They were just as beautiful as the living room. It was plain to see that Earl was very rich.

Back in the living room Earl said, "You want to freshen up?"

Bobby Jo nodded.

"Take a bath if you like."

Ten minutes later, Bobby Jo was luxuriating in a bubble bath in a sunken tub. She felt wonderful.

Earl was standing by the bar when she came into the living room. He was wearing a beautiful satin jacket and looked terrific. She hoped she looked good. She was wearing one of the dresses he had bought for her and had her hair piled up and tied. She had also applied some makeup, and when he looked at her there was no doubt that he was attracted to her. That made her feel very good.

"You one fine-looking woman," he said.

She sat down on a stool at the bar.

"Tom Collins okay?" Earl asked.

Bobby Jo said yes, but she had no idea what he was talking about until he made the drink. He was having some sort of whiskey in a short glass filled with ice cubes.

She sipped the Tom Collins. It tasted just like some sort of tart soda, not bad at all. She felt very grown-up.

After she had drunk about half of it she noticed that it made her able to say everything that was on her mind easily.

"So tell me," she said, "what business can you help me with?"

"That's a surprise, remember?" Earl said. "Let's relax now."

They relaxed. Bobby Jo gave him more details on her life, being careful not to say anything that would give away her age. Earl was a very good listener.

She had another drink. Never in her life had she felt calmer or more in control. The things in the room and Earl's face seemed somehow to be clearer than anything had ever been in her life. Her mind was super-sharp.

So she was surprised when she got off the stool to shift her position and had just a little bit of trouble with her balance.

She wanted to tell Earl that she wasn't used to drinking but said nothing.

Earl prepared them both new drinks—her third—and then put on some music. It was something she had never heard before, something about pledging love, but she liked the sound. It made her feel sad and happy at the same time.

She looked at Earl. His eyes were so large and dark. Beautiful.

"You want to dance, little lady?"

She felt something spurt inside her. "Yes."

Then she was on the carpet with him, dancing very slowly, her shoes off, feeling her heart hammer. Both her arms were wrapped around his body, which felt very lean and hard, and he smelled good, so very, very good.

When the song was over he just stood there. He looked down in her eyes and took her face in his hands. "Pretty little child," he said.

And then he kissed her, and she found herself responding, wanting to please him, to do anything he wanted so he would be happy with her and take care of her.

He carried her into his bedroom and closed the door behind them. It was dim.

Bobby Jo felt herself wanting him desperately as he slowly undressed her. She seemed so agitated, so crazy; through a haze of desire it occurred to her that he seemed so in control. She liked that.

Soon, she was standing there nude, and he stripped off and carefully laid his clothes on a chair.

He had his back to her, and when he turned and walked toward the bed she gasped. They had jokes in school about how big colored guys were. It was true, and she liked the idea very, very much. It made her feel very small. She loved the feeling.

She wanted to love him. She wanted to love him to death.

He drove her crazy. She was going wild, and he was so methodical. She had the feeling that he just wanted to drive her out of her mind. She thrust her pelvis up, meeting his thrusts with a ferocity that surprised her. She wanted to break him down, make him gasp like Daddy did, like Steve had, but she couldn't. He was in total control, even when he orgasmed inside her. She loved it.

They stayed in bed until early afternoon, and then he told her that he had to go out—alone—and she was deeply disappointed. She wanted him to be with her. She needed him, but after he had said no once she found herself unable to ask him again.

"You stay here," he said. "I'll be back. Late. Help yourself to any food. Watch TV. Be a good girl."

It should have been a nice day for Bobby Jo. Earl had a color TV—the first Bobby Jo had ever really watched— and she spent the day watching cartoons, *Sky King*, *Kukla*, *Fran, and Ollie*, and other of her favorite programs that her mother sometimes wouldn't let her watch.

But her mind was constantly on Earl.

When darkness came, Bobby Jo went into the bedroom and tried to sleep. But she couldn't. All she could think about was Earl and that he wasn't there.

Earl meant what he said. He would be home late. He came into the bedroom where Bobby Jo had been trying to sleep when the light of dawn was starting to fill the room.

A minute after Earl entered the room she could smell alcohol. It reminded her of Daddy. Daddy and alcohol meant sex.

But Earl surprised—and disappointed—her. He lay down beside her but did not touch her.

She touched him.

"Not now, baby. Go to sleep."

Bobby Jo wanted to argue. But she said nothing. Above

all, she did not want to annoy Earl. He meant too much to her.

It took her a long time, but she was finally able to get to sleep.

When Bobby Jo awakened later in the day, she didn't know where she was for a moment, then realized she was in Earl's bedroom and that it was almost five o'clock. Earl was not in the bed, but she heard the shower in the bathroom down the hall.

Five minutes later he came into the room with only a towel wrapped around him.

He came over to the bed and sat down next to Bobby Jo. "How you doin', baby?"

"Okay."

He leaned over and kissed her on the mouth. "You got time for a little lovin'?"

She nodded. She had been ready since she awakened.

"I got the time too."

Later, they lay in bed, Earl smoking and Bobby Jo trying to.

"Remember I told you, Bobby Jo, that I may be able to help you out?"

"Yes."

"Tonight I'm going to do that."

Bobby Jo sat up. "What is it?"

"I'll tell you on the way."

They left the apartment an hour later, both looking, Bobby Jo thought, terrific. Earl was in a very sharp suit and wore a beautiful fur hat, while she was in one of the outfits—a sequinned mini-skirt and short coat—that Earl had bought her.

She even caught the old doorman sneaking a look at her behind.

She was in for another surprise: Earl had a car, a beautiful white Cadillac that was parked near the front of the building. Bobby Jo got in. Earl pulled away from the curb. It was quiet, beautiful, smooth.

Bobby Jo wondered where they were going, but she said nothing to Earl.

A few minutes later she was still thinking about their destination when Earl spoke. "You were wondering about how I'm going to help you, right, Bobby Jo?"

Bobby Jo nodded.

"By you going on dates. I operate a dating service, and you goin' to be one of the girls that go on dates."

"With who?"

"Different people. I introduce you to 'em."

"Where do we go. What do we do."

"The date takes care of everything. You go wherever he wants to go."

"Like to the movies?"

Earl smiled broadly.

"Yeah, maybe. To the movies. And then when I get paid, you get paid. Everybody's happy. Okay?"

Earl was watching her carefully. It made Bobby Jo nervous. "All right."

Earl stopped the car at 50th Street and Tenth Avenue, facing south.

Bobby Jo was getting more nervous. She didn't know what to expect. But she wanted to please Earl.

"When the date is over, he'll pay you. Then you bring all the money back to me. Okay?"

"Sure."

Then they simply waited, and watched. She sensed that Earl didn't want to talk with her now so she kept quiet.

She tried but couldn't shake the nervousness. She thought of Sport, her teddy bear. But she couldn't have taken him on the date with her. There was no place to hide him.

"There's your date," Earl said.

Bobby Jo followed his line of sight. A big black limousine was pulling up to the curb across the street.

"Okay, Bobby Jo. You have a good time. See you later."

She turned to Earl. He was smiling. She went out the door.

As she crossed the street the rear window slid down and a face appeared. It was of a very fat old man. He was smiling.

The last thought that Bobby Jo had before getting into the limousine was that he was probably the father of her date.

CHAPTER 15

JUNE 16, 1962, 8:00 A.M.

It took Bobby Jo a couple of weeks of working for Earl before she learned what she was doing. One of Earl's other ladies told her, and it really made the lady laugh.

"You a ho, child," she said, "Earl turned you out, the way he turned me and all his other ladies out."

The revelation scared and enraged Bobby Jo, but then Earl had explained it all to her. He told her that, yes, she was now one of his ladies, but that that was something to be very proud of and that he, Earl, would always be there to care for her. He would protect her and love her, and when the time came for her to leave the Life, which is what he called it, he would be there to help her, to make sure she was fine.

Bobby Jo chose to believe him. She went to work with a single-minded dedication and got to be known as the star of Earl's stable. On some nights she would turn twenty tricks, double what was normal.

Earl was very proud of her, and Bobby Jo basked in the glory. She liked the thick envy she could see coming off the other girls. She felt special and loved.

All was not perfect, though. The work was hard. Some of the johns were dirty, and a lot of them were drunk or spaced out, and you had to watch for disease.

And it could be dangerous. There were some freaks who got off on hurting girls.

Bobby Jo wouldn't allow it. When she sensed it coming she would get herself out of the situation one way or another. A couple of months after she went on the stroll she started carrying a knife, and she knew she would use it if she had to. In fact, she would sort of like it, just cutting some fucker who was trying to hurt her.

She had heard one story of a dude in Harlem who tried to work a girl over and she cut his cock off with a straight razor. Fine. The fucker deserved that.

The sex itself didn't bother Bobby Jo. It was a physical act and meant nothing more to her than that. When some chump was groaning above her she might as well have been filing her nails.

Generally she felt happy. It was an exciting life, particularly when Earl would invite her and maybe one or two other ladies to his apartment for special parties. And there were always the late-night gatherings with Earl and the other ladies in the particular bar that Earl was hanging out in at the time. And she was always the star.

But there were some moments of sadness. From out of the blue and at any moment a scene would flash in her mind of her and her father doing something together happily in her childhood, or even her with both Momma and Daddy: a moment from an animal farm . . . the light shining on their faces from candles on a birthday cake of

106

long ago . . . the way Daddy used to hug her before all the other stuff began.

But the moments would fade.

Mostly, Bobby Jo thought about Earl. He was the center of her existence, the man she relied on and turned to in times of trouble; the man who would always care for Bobby Jo.

The trouble began when the nigger Felice—or Lice, as the ladies nicknamed her—came along.

She was fifteen, but with a body like a Cadillac, built as well or better than Bobby Jo. Walking down the block, her body packed in a sequinned mini-skirt tight as a sausage skin and her hair in a huge shiny beehive, she could really make heads turn.

It made Bobby Jo jealous when she saw her, and even more jealous when Earl invited Lice to stay at his apartment. Normally, the girls lived together in an apartment "hotel"—more a rattrap than anything—off West 45th Street, and except for partying at Earl's they never stayed there.

Then Earl did something else that increased the animosity toward Lice—and Earl. He started her doing bottom woman work, taking applications and helping him turn out new hos.

Normally, this was the province of Marcie. She had been Earl's girlfriend fifteen years earlier and had in fact been his ticket to the Life: she was the first woman he had ever turned out.

The other ladies were silent about Lice—at least to Earl. Marcie was not. She complained bitterly to Earl about Lice doing her work. Earl told her not to meddle. He would take care of business.

But Marcie, everyone knew, loved Earl and one day

hoped to settle down with him. Somewhere in a little private place inside her he had never stopped being her boyfriend. All the girls knew that.

Marcie started to drink, and then, one night in a fit of stoned-out rage, went for Lice—and Earl went for Marcie with pimp sticks—wire hangers wrapped tightly together.

He beat her so bad she ended up in the hospital, and when Bobby Jo went to visit her she cried. Marcie's face was blown up like a balloon, and it was painful for her to move.

Marcie cried, too, and Bobby Jo knew all too well it was more than the physical pain Marcie was crying about. It was what Earl did, what it meant, that hurt her. Earl had given her the Big Lie: he didn't care about her at all, and all those years that she had been loyal and loving to the motherfucker meant nothing. It told Bobby Jo everything she ever wanted to know about Earl Watkins.

And more. Looking at Marcie in the bed Bobby Jo thought she looked much older than the thirty-one she said she was. She looked forty, and her figure was gone, and there was something else gone that Bobby Jo couldn't quite put her finger on for a while, and then she did: something had died inside Marcie; there was a terrible sense of lostness about her.

The sight chilled Bobby Jo. This was the Life. This was how it ended, in some hospital bed all used up, and the only thing you knew how to do was fuck and suck; it was not hard to imagine how Marcie would end up: working the West Side piers as a five-dollar bandit until her luck ran out.

No way, Bobby Jo thought, no way was she going to end up like this. Fuck that nigger.

Bobby Jo resolved to get out. She knew it was a very

dangerous enterprise. The last thing you wanted to get caught at was going on the fly from a pimp. That was a killing offense, and Bobby Jo could see Earl was capable of it.

So she bided her time, plotting how to do it, not even thinking about how she would survive outside the Life, but knowing she had to get out.

She talked shit to Earl, hiding it all behind a smiling face, waiting for a chance to make her run, figuring out how to do it so she was never likely to see Earl again.

Then, another pimp solved her problem. He stabbed Earl to death outside the Blue Flame Bar on West 48th Street.

One of the other ladies told Bobby Jo that Earl had lost a lot of blood before he died, so the day after he was killed they visited the site. Bloodstains were still clearly visible. She and the other lady stared at them for a while, and then Bobby Jo said, "Hey, Earl, how you doin'?"

Then she and the other lady walked over the stains, because they would have gotten arrested pissing on them.

Bobby Jo knew she had to move fast. There would be other pimps trying to catch her.

She did. Working fourteen-hour days on her own, she had, at the end of five days, over seven hundred dollars.

On the sixth day, the first pimp tried to catch her, making a light pass at her. But Bobby Jo knew the pressure would continue.

Two hours after the hit, Bobby Jo was standing on the 42nd Street subway platform waiting for the uptown train.

She was dressed in the most conservative outfit she had, and strapped to her waist was the money. She had left all her other clothing in the apartment, as if she was coming back.

Now, as she waited for the train, she felt nervous but good. She felt sure she could put the Life behind her, but if she ever needed to make a few dollars she knew she could do that too.

In the bag she carried she had cosmetics, tissues, and the myriad other things any woman carried.

Plus Sport. Sometimes, she still liked to hold him in her arms when she went to bed.

The tracks clicked, and a minute later the uptown train thundered into the station.

She got on the train. It lurched and started uptown to, Bobby Jo just knew, a new life.

CHAPTER 16

Outside the building the temperature was 82, and the weatherman had said that it would be close to 100. Inside the building Bobby Jo Johnson thought it was almost as cold as Cleveland.

Inside was Goldman's Ice Cream Company in the Riverdale section of the Bronx. Bobby Jo, dressed in a white smock and with a jaunty little cap on her head, was watching a single line of chocolate-covered ice cream bars go by on a conveyor belt. When she saw one that was damaged she would pick it up, strip the paper off, then flick the ice cream into one stainless steel garbage can and drop the stick in another.

During the past two weeks, since she had started the job, she had done a variety of jobs in the factory. All were boring beyond belief, but it was better than working for a pimp.

The job had been easy to get. She had lied about her age, and no one questioned it.

111

She figured, when she first started, that she would go for some other kind of job in a couple of months, but she knew now she was going to have to change fairly fast. Not that she was financially pressed. She made eighty dollars and change a week, plus she had a cheap rented room and had put around six hundred and fifty dollars in the bank. It was just that she knew the job would drive her crazy.

But what kind of job should she get?

The streets had taught her some things, and one was to maximize your strong points. Take the best thing you had and sell it.

That, of course, was her looks. She had to get into some line of work where her looks could do her some good.

For two Sundays now, she had carefully gone over the want-ad listings in the papers. At first, she didn't know what she was looking for, but then she saw the ads for receptionists and waitresses. Waitresses, she knew, could make good money; she figured receptionists could too. She remembered one receptionist she saw at Dr. Mendoza's office, where she had gone a few months earlier to find out about a rash she had. That girl—her name was Alice—was very pretty.

She decided to focus on those jobs. After another week or so she would call in sick one day; she would have all the job interviews lined up.

Promptly at ten o'clock a horn blared for the morning break. As usual, she went into the small, battered place the employees called the lunchroom. In it were ten battered tables with equally battered chairs. Food supplies were provided by three vending machines, one that dispensed soda, another candy bars, and another watered-down soup and coffee that was always regular no matter what selection you made.

As usual, Bobby Jo had brought her lunch, a salami and cheese sandwich. She bought a bottle of Pepsi and sat down at one of the tables.

The employees in the lunchroom—all dressed in white uniforms—were not unfriendly, but not particularly friendly either. Everyone seemed so tired all the time, and their eyes showed nothing. Nodding hello seemed an effort.

She ate her sandwich slowly, occasionally sipping on the soda, and she gradually became aware, out of the side of her eye, that someone was watching her.

She turned and nailed him. She had seen him watching her before. He was a guy who seemed fairly old—maybe thirty—and he had on only street clothes and no hat: he was a supervisor of some sort; they didn't wear uniforms. Bobby Jo thought she had seen him in a big glassed-in corner office.

His face colored, but he tried to rally. He smiled, got up, and headed toward Bobby Jo's table carrying a lunchbox. He came up to her.

He reminded her of a shy John.

"Is anyone sitting here?" he asked.

Bobby Jo shook her head.

"May I?"

Bobby Jo shrugged.

He sat down, carefully setting the lunchbox on the table. "My name is Albert Brooks," he said. "What's yours?"

"Bobby Jo Johnson."

"That's an interesting name."

Bobby Jo worked on her sandwich. He was not, she thought, very good-looking. In fact, he was homely. He had a big nose, thick lips, a very high forehead with thinnish blond hair, and very blue eyes.

"How long have you worked here?" Brooks asked.

113

"Two weeks."

"You work on the line?"

"Yeah."

Brooks had opened his lunchbox, and from it had taken a plastic soup bowl. He carefully removed the lid. It was not soup, but some sort of stew. Bobby Jo sniffed a pleasant aroma. It had been a week since she had had a hot meal. There was nothing in her room for making a meal, just a thing you could stick into water to make it hot.

"Would you like some of this?"

"I don't have anything to put it in."

Brooks smiled. He had a nice smile.

He reached into his lunchbox and from it took an empty plastic bowl, a spoon, and a napkin. "I always carry a spare," he said. "People like this stew."

Oh, Bobby Jo thought. *What kind of a chump is this? He comes ready to give his lunch away.*

Then she thought, *When is he going to make his move?*

She carefully ladled a bit into her mouth. It was warm without being hot—and delicious.

She glanced up. Brooks was watching her. He had pale white skin, and she could see his cheeks redden. She had seen the look before and recognized it right away. He was getting hot. She finished the stew, alternately biting into the sandwich. It was a delicious combination. For a moment, she thought of school lunches, soup and sandwiches, a crowded, noisy cafeteria. . . . That seemed forever ago.

"Where you from?" Brooks asked.

"Huntington, Long Island."

"Oh. I know that," Brooks said.

"Out on the north shore of the island. Forty miles or so, right?"

"Right," Bobby Jo said.

114

"You come all the way in from there every day?"

"I got a room in the Bronx."

"I live in the Bronx too," Brooks said. "Where'd you work before this?"

"Downtown. I was a receptionist in a doctor's office."

"You type?"

The street had made Bobby Jo a glib liar. "No. You didn't have to."

"But you're familiar with paperwork?"

"Sure."

Brooks nodded. "You know," he said, "I'm looking for someone to help me in the office. Would you be interested in that?"

Bobby Jo looked at him. She could see her look was doing things to him. She had him. She played with him.

"What does the job involve?" she asked.

"Well, it's just answering phones, a little paperwork, and some typing."

"I told you, I don't type."

"I know. But it's not a lot of typing. You could pick that up."

"I wouldn't want to take a job that was too big for me."

"I appreciate that," Brooks said. "I appreciate that very much. But you wouldn't, I assure you."

Bobby Jo took the last spoonful of stew and the last bite of sandwich. Brooks was busy eating, but she could sense a certain tenseness coming off, almost like a smell.

She swallowed. "I could give it a try."

Brooks beamed broadly. "Good. Great. We could start you tomorrow."

Bobby Jo paused. She frowned. He looked scared. "I didn't even ask you how much the job pays."

"Oh, more than you're making now. A hundred dollars a week and change."

"Sounds okay."

"Good. Good." Brooks finished the last of his stew.

Bobby Jo wondered what he was going to do next. In the bottom of his lunchbox was a banana. It was just too much.

Brooks picked up the banana. "Would you like this?"

Wordlessly, Bobby Jo took it, peeled it, and ate it very slowly. She could swear that Brooks's face changed color four times as she ate. Inside, she screamed with glee. When she finally handed the skin back to him she was dead sure that he wouldn't be able to stand up without something else also standing up.

Ha-ha.

CHAPTER 17

A week after she started working in the office, Albert Brooks asked Bobby Jo to go out to the movies.

She knew he was going to make some move. He couldn't seem to keep his eyes off her.

She didn't say yes right away. She played with him, telling him she didn't know if it was right that they go out right away. "After all, we've only known each other a short while."

She couldn't keep from laughing when she thought of what Albert might think if he saw her all decked out and on the stroll.

Albert seemed to like her reluctance, but it didn't stop him from asking. He practically got down on his knees.

She waited until the end of the second week before she said yes. Albert was a total puppy dog by then. She thought his joy was so great he was going to cry.

They went out on a Saturday night.

Albert was very formal, all dressed up in a tweed jacket

and plain pants and with a bow tie on. He was not the world's sharpest dresser.

But he was a gentleman, which was okay. He reminded her, more than anything, of one of those college kids who used to come down for their first piece of tail: at the beginning they were all shy and retiring, but at the end their dicks were hard and what they wanted more than anything was a blow job.

When the time came, Albert would be like that too.

He had a nice car, a brand-new 1962 Impala. It wasn't Earl's Cadillac, but it was a nice car.

As the night went on, Bobby Jo almost laughed at just how much of a gentleman Albert was. He insisted on opening and closing doors for her, he said please and thank you—he just seemed more like her servant than a date.

Maybe, Bobby Jo thought, he was into S&M. Time would tell.

After the movie they went to La Luna, a little Italian restaurant in the Arthur Avenue section of the Bronx.

While they ate, Bobby Jo learned more about Albert Brooks.

He was twenty-eight and had never been married. He lived alone in a private house on Valentine Avenue just south of 198th Street. Until six months ago his mother had been alive, and since she had been an invalid during the last three years of her life, Albert didn't have much of a private life; he was either at work or taking care of her.

He said he was an only child and that his mother had been a widow a long time. His father had gone down with a ship in World War II.

When he said that, he hesitated, and Bobby Jo swore he was going to cry. Over what?

He said that he had been working at Goldman's since high school, and that he figured that in a year, two at the most, he would be invited by the Goldman brothers—who owned the company—to take an executive position "inside" —off the factory floor.

About halfway through the meal the inevitable questions about her own life started. Bobby Jo was ready. She had prepared an entire life history for the fuzz and polished it over the months she spent on the stroll.

She had learned that a lie that is partially true is always the best, so she told him that she had left her home because of trouble with her mother and father—drinking— and that was about that.

As she expected, Albert didn't question her further; he seemed, more than anything, to be concerned about her. He was funny.

After dinner, they stood outside the restaurant. It was cool and pleasant, and Bobby Jo felt good, slightly tipsy from the wine.

Albert looked at her. "I can take you home," he said, "or if you'd like, I can show you my home."

Bobby Jo smiled at him. "I'd love to see your home."

The house was on a corner, and it seemed to be the most impressive on the block. It was old-fashioned-looking— not like her house—and it was very tall and had a front porch.

The inside was old-fashioned too, Albert took her on a tour of the rooms, and they seemed to be from another time; they reminded her of rooms she had seen once on a school trip to a museum. They were clean—very clean— but old.

"This is a really nice house," Bobby Jo said when they

got back to the living room, where they had started their tour.

"Thank you. My family is the original owner, and it's the only place I've ever lived. It was passed down from one generation to the next."

Albert went over to an old rocking chair that was next to and facing the window. "This is where my mother used to sit," he said softly, "until very near the end."

"It must have been hard," Bobby Jo said.

Albert smiled slightly but said nothing. He went over to a fireplace with a mantel on top. On it was a picture of a man in a sailor's uniform. The man looked a lot like Albert. He picked it up. "This is my father. He was quite a guy."

He looked at the picture a long time, then replaced it on the mantel. He smiled at Bobby Jo. "Would you like some coffee and cake?"

"Sure," she said.

She felt something warm surge inside but thought, *What the fuck is with this guy. When is he going to make his move?*

Ten minutes later they were sitting in the dining room having coffee and cake. The cake was delicious.

"This is scrumptious," she said.

"I baked it myself," Albert said.

Following coffee, he said, "How about some ice cream?"

Bobby Jo smiled. After two weeks at Goldman's she figured she'd never eat ice cream again. But she surprised herself. She felt like some.

Albert surprised and delighted her when he took out the ice cream. It was Sealtest brand.

Bobby Jo laughed, and so did Albert.

"I show Sealtest, but I serve only the best," Albert

said, and he put the package of Sealtest—which was empty—back in the freezer and took out three half gallons of Goldman's, from which Bobby Jo chose chocolate.

"I played the trick on the Goldman brothers once," Albert said as they ate the ice cream. "Only Bernie laughed, but fortunately he owns the most stock."

Bobby Jo helped Albert clean up, then they went into the living room.

"Would you like to look at some of my family albums?" Albert asked.

Bobby Jo said that she would—and she did.

For a half hour they sat on the couch looking at album after album of family pictures. It had been a happy family, Bobby Jo could see. It was as if they were all happy together and they took a lot of pictures to remember how it was.

Bobby Jo remembered. There were very few pictures of herself, her mother, and her father. When she was a toddler was about it. Maybe they didn't want to remember.

Bobby Jo remembered one and it made her angry. She was in a bathing suit, about two, and was on her father's shoulders. She wondered what he had been fucking thinking about.

She wondered then, when Albert was going to make the pass. They were on the couch. This was the right time. What was he waiting for?

But he didn't, and she started to sense he wasn't going to. Then his statement confirmed it.

"It's getting kind of late," he said. "Why don't I take you home."

"Okay." Bobby Jo felt a surge of anger at Albert. She was mad that he hadn't made a pass.

As it happened, his "pass" came outside her room.

He drove her home, then walked her to the door. He stood there uncomfortably, and even in the semidarkness she swore she could see his cheeks go red.

"May I," he said, his voice a little squeaky, "kiss you good night?"

Bobby Jo did not answer. She simply stepped forward, took his head in her hands, and they kissed gently.

"Thank you," he said, "for a wonderful evening."

"It was my pleasure," Bobby Jo said. And she meant it.

Later, lying on her bed in the darkness in her tiny room, Bobby Jo held Sport close and thought about how Albert had kissed her and she realized that she had wanted to be kissed like that all her life. The kiss was like a movie kiss, and it came from someplace deep inside Albert and was meant for only her, only her.

It was so different from the way her father kissed her, hurting her mouth, and with his tongue deep inside, and then the men who fucked her. A kiss was just something that came before them sticking their cock in her ass or her cunt or mouth.

She pictured Albert. Serving cake, his ears sticking out, almost with tears in his eyes when he talked about his father, caring for his mother.

This guy was something valuable. She closed her eyes and squeezed Sport close to her. Tears formed in her eyes. For the first time in a very long time, she didn't feel alone.

CHAPTER 18

For the next three months, Albert and Bobby Jo went out three or four nights a week, and Bobby Jo got to know Albert Brooks real well. He was no different than he had been that first night with her: almost too good to be true.

Then, on a lovely, cool day in late October, they were walking through the Botanical Gardens in the Bronx and Albert seemed especially quiet. Bobby Jo knew why he was quiet.

She was not surprised when he asked her to marry him, and this time she didn't play around. This time she said yes right away.

They were married on a lovely day in late November by a justice of the peace in Yonkers, with Albert's friend Lou Seaman and his wife, Charlotte, attending. Bobby Jo saw it as the beginning of a new life for her. It was as if the past was dead and gone forever, the tricks and the pimps and the drugs and, before that, her father, using and abusing her—all this could be buried forever under an avalanche of love. She was no longer Bobby Jo Johnson. Her name was Bobby Jo Brooks.

Everything went like a breeze at the ceremony, and after it was over they drove down to La Luna, which had become their special place, and Lou and Charlotte surprised them with a small, delicious cake prepared by the La Luna chef that, Lou said, had about a million calories per piece.

They had a full seven-course meal, complete with antipasto, all washed down with La Luna's good house wine.

As they ate and drank, Bobby Jo, as subtly as she could, watched Albert, and wondered about him.

Was he, indeed, too good to be true? Was he a wolf in sheep's clothing?

Was there something bad about him that she was not seeing?

Did he think he could control her, hurt her, and get away with it?

Throughout all this thinking, Bobby Jo smiled, hiding the anger, and at one point was even on the verge of saying to Albert, "Are you too good to be true, Albert? Are you a fuck, like other men?"

But she didn't, and after a while the bad feelings went away, and then she was smiling from deep inside and realized how lucky she was to have Albert. She had never met anyone in her life like him.

They would live a long and happy life together.

Outside the restaurant Lou and Charlotte bade them goodbye and they went back to Albert's—their—house, where he insisted on carrying Bobby Jo across the threshold. It was, she thought, just like in the movies.

The next day, they were to leave on a honeymoon to Florida, but tonight, the first night of their married life, they were to spend at home—their home.

They drank some more wine and then went up to the bedroom.

Bobby Jo had bought a new white nightgown which, somehow, reflected the way she felt about everything, and a new perfume: Intimate.

As she walked into the bedroom, where Albert was already waiting under the covers, Bobby Jo felt as good as she ever had in her life. There was just Albert and her, this moment, no yesterday, no tomorrow, just now in the soft light in a room with a man who loved her utterly.

She slipped under the covers.

"My God," Albert said, and he sounded like he had tears in his eyes, "you have made me so happy. I have waited so, so long for someone like you to come into my life. Thank you, my darling."

More than once over their courting period, Bobby Jo had wondered about Albert's lovemaking. She found out: there was nothing wrong with it. He was gentle and caring and totally loving. He was also insatiable. He could not get enough of her.

Bobby Jo responded, but she controlled herself. The last thing she wanted was for Albert to know she was experienced. Maybe someday, but not tonight. Tonight was her chance to be a virgin again, a virgin in white.

They made love all night, and once, Bobby Jo thought she came close to coming. She realized that coming was a little problem with her now—not even Earl had been able to accomplish that the last few times they did it—but with Albert she had come pretty close. She felt sure she would solve that problem as time went by.

In the morning, the sun had risen before they stopped making love.

She heard Albert's voice through a pleasant downward drift toward sleep.

"Who knows, darling?" he said. "Maybe God will bless us tonight with a child."

The idea scared Bobby Jo for a moment, but then she felt fine.

"Would you want a boy or a girl?" she asked.

"I don't care, honey, just as long as you and the baby are all right."

Bobby Jo's last thought before drifting into sleep was that she hoped she did get pregnant, and that for Albert's sake she hoped it would be a boy.

CHAPTER 19

Albert Brooks got his wish. Just about three months to the day after they were married Bobby Jo learned she was pregnant. Albert's response could fairly be described as ecstatic.

"God, Bobby Jo," he told her, "all down through the years I was hoping that one day this big house could fill up again—fill up with love. That I would meet someone like you, and that we could have children. I never dreamed it would all come true."

Bobby Jo was happy too. She wasn't thinking about any of the bad stuff of the past, and she was handling the role of homemaker—she had quit her job at Goldman's—very well. She had had lots of practice.

Albert was incredibly attentive to Bobby Jo. During the first few months of her pregnancy her stomach hadn't swollen at all, but Albert acted as if she were waddling around.

For those first few months Bobby Jo didn't see any changes, except for her periods stopping, and she didn't feel anything either. She started to wonder if she were actually pregnant.

Then, around the beginning of the fourth month, she started to feel sick in the morning. She went to the doctor.

"It's nothing," he said. "Just normal morning sickness. Don't worry about it."

It was not worrisome to Bobby Jo—just sickening. And she found, as it continued, that she started to feel resentful toward Albert. More than resentful. Angry. It was Albert who had caused this.

She tried, as much as possible, to control her feelings, but as time went by she found she couldn't control them completely and started to snipe at Albert: at the TV programs he watched, the papers and magazines he read, the fact that he always smelled sweet, like the factory—just anything.

Albert didn't understand why she was mad at him, and he was hurt by it.

Tough shit, Bobby Jo thought. He could be such an asshole.

The sickness continued through her fourth and fifth months, getting even worse. It occasionally progressed from a nauseous feeling in the pit of her stomach to actually throwing up. She found that smells that she ordinarily liked, like bacon and eggs and toast, made her sick.

And, above all, she found herself loathing the smell of Goldman's on Albert. It got so he was bathing once a day and constantly laundering his clothes.

Then, there were Albert's sexual demands. He was like a rabbit, Bobby Jo thought. Never mind that her stomach was swelling and she felt like sex about as much as she felt like throwing up.

One day she simply stopped it. She told Albert in no

uncertain terms that sex was over until after the baby was born.

"But it won't hurt you or the baby," Albert said. "I asked the doctor."

"The fucking doctor," Bobby Jo said, "doesn't know everything. I know my body."

So it stopped.

Despite all this, Bobby Jo still believed she loved Albert, and the pregnancy was certainly not without joyous moments.

There was, for example, the first time she felt the baby move. She was walking across the kitchen and felt a little thump inside her. For a moment, she thought it was gas, but then realized what it was. That night she and Albert sat on the couch, her maternity smock lifted up to expose her bare swollen belly, and watched the baby move.

At the beginning of the sixth month, the doctor told Bobby Jo and Albert something that was scary, at least at first. She was going to have a breach birth.

But the doctor reassured them. "A breach birth," he said, "simply means that the baby is born feet, rather than head, first. As long as we know about it, we can deal with it."

"How?" Albert asked.

"There are certain drugs Mrs. Brooks can take, and when the baby is being born we're able to guide it out fine."

"Is there any danger?"

"Hardly any," the doctor said. "In the most exaggerated situation we could always perform a cesarean section."

The information from the doctor increased Albert's babying of Bobby Jo. She could hardly do anything without him wanting to do it for her, and he was constantly reassuring her that everything would be all right.

The morning sickness returned in the seventh month, the worst month of her pregnancy. And adding to her woe was that over the previous months she had gained around thirty pounds, and she had difficulty moving around.

Gastric distress of one sort or another seemed to be a permanent part of her life.

And despite what the doctor had said, she worried about a breach birth.

She read one article—or half an article—about breach births that really scared her. She told the doctor about it and he poo-poohed it.

"Do yourself a favor," he said. "Don't read medical articles in magazines."

Still, Bobby Jo wondered—and found that there seemed to be a constant anger simmering in her against Albert. Not only was pregnancy hard, but it would probably ruin her figure too.

In the eighth month the sickness lifted, and with it, to a large degree, her anger toward Albert.

In the ninth month, the sickness returned a bit; Bobby Jo swore to herself that she would never have a child again.

As the time came for her to give birth—she was expecting in the middle of August—she and Albert made plans about what they would do if she started to go into labor when Albert was at the office. He had recently gotten the inside job he had so coveted.

The arrangement was simple: if he was at work, Bobby Jo would call him; if his line was busy, she could contact Lou Seaman, who also worked at Goldman's.

Bobby Jo felt the first contraction on the morning of

June 20. She called the doctor, who told her to head for the hospital when the pains were ten minutes apart.

She waited until the pains were fifteen minutes apart before calling Albert. She got right through. He said he was heading home immediately.

Almost immediately after she called, the time between pains dropped greatly. This only mildly worried her.

But her worry increased when Albert did not arrive within the fifteen or twenty minutes it normally took him to drive home from Goldman's.

Bobby Jo called the factory. Albert had left, she was told, a half hour earlier.

Where the fuck was he? Bobby Jo thought.

Maybe he had car trouble, or an accident. He would call if he had car trouble.

She had called from the bedroom and went from there to the front window to watch for Albert.

But there was no Albert, and soon Bobby Jo became aware that the pains were only three minutes or so apart.

Where was he? Where was he? She was scared and enraged at the same time.

She was sitting on the bed when she felt a warm sensation between her legs and for a horrific moment thought she was bleeding. But it was her water; her water had broken.

It shocked her into action.

She dialed the operator, and a half minute later she was on the phone with a policeman.

"Hang on, lady, we're coming."

And come they did.

Two minutes after she called she heard the wail of a siren getting closer.

She put a coat on over her soaked housedress and waddled out to the front of the house.

Tears streamed down her face. Tears of pain, of fear, of rage.

Where, God, where was Albert?

Then she was being hustled into the police car by a young, dark-haired cop who looked as old as she was and another who was only slightly older.

"Hang on, lady, we'll have you to the hospital in no time."

The pains were coming now in cruel rhythms. She got into the back of the police car, the older cop beside her, and the car burned rubber pulling away from the curb.

They were only seven or eight minutes from the hospital, Misericordia.

Then, through the pain came a terrifying sensation—she could feel the baby moving. She gritted her teeth and held on.

"Oh Jesus," she cried. "Oh Jesus, I can't stop it."

"Hold on, lady, hold on," the cop who was in the back with her said.

"I can't, I can't."

She felt something coming out of her. She had to hold it. It was a breach. The baby would die, she would die, Albert would die.

She held, held, held.

Then something came out.

"Step on it, Charlie," the young cop said. He was looking down, his face a mask of concern.

Bobby Jo hiked herself up and looked down over the mound of her belly.

God. She could see a little bloody foot.

*   *   *

One of the nurses later said that the doctor had earned his money. He had to do a risky high forceps delivery, but was able to do it perfectly. Neither the baby nor Bobby Jo suffered any harm.

It was a boy, just like Bobby Jo wanted. Eight pounds, four ounces, and his name, as they had decided, was Albert III.

The doctor had anesthetized Bobby Jo, and when she came out of it the fear started to clutch at her. Albert had not shown up yet. Something must have happened. Something bad. He just wasn't like this.

In mid-afternoon, Lou Seaman came into the room unannounced. He looked very serious, and when he got close Bobby Jo saw that his eyes had tears in them.

Oh God.

Albert Brooks had died—or more accurately had been killed—on the same day his son was born.

It was a traffic accident, Bobby Jo learned, on the Bronx River Parkway. No other car was involved; Albert had apparently lost control and hammered into a telephone pole. Death was instantaneous.

Bobby Jo was heavily sedated by the doctor, but the grief bore through. Lying there in the hospital bed at twilight with her baby in her arms, Bobby Jo could feel an aching emptiness, a terrible sense that something had been torn from her that could never be replaced. For she realized, totally and completely, that as long as she lived the likes of Albert Brooks would never come her way again.

Tears rolled down her cheeks, but after a while, she stopped, and looked carefully at the baby, who was nursing off her.

He was blond and blue-eyed, just like her. He had beautiful features—and Albert's ears.

She would always have him, Bobby Jo thought, and just at that moment the baby seemed to look up at her.

She looked away. Even with the sedative in her, her heart rate increased and she felt a hollowness in her stomach.

The baby had scared her.

CHAPTER 20

There was a frown on Bobby Jo Brook's face. She was thinking of little Albert. If it wasn't for him she would be able to party all night, which is exactly what she felt like doing.

She was in McGrath's bar on Central Avenue in Yonkers with Lloyd Gibbs, whom she considered one of the handsomest guys she had ever seen. He had large blue eyes, dark wavy hair, and flashing white teeth. And his body! He worked in construction in Manhattan on big buildings. Bobby Jo didn't think there was an ounce of fat on him, something she had checked as recently as four hours earlier, when they had started the night in the Shady Rest Motel by the Bronx Zoo, a hot-bed motel that they visited at least once a week.

It was only 1:00 A.M., and Bobby Jo was just getting warmed up. She was ready to dance up a storm, and then go to either of their places for some more fun, but the babysitter had told her that she had to leave by 1:30, so Bobby Jo would have to leave very soon. Otherwise the babysitter might get mad and not come again.

Bobby Jo was having difficulty getting a good babysitter. She had started going out ten months ago, and during that time had had five babysitters.

One reason was that she was late all the time; she didn't come home when she promised, and word in the neighborhood—she still lived in the house where she and Albert had lived—had spread.

But the other reason was little Albert. A couple of the babysitters had complained that he was extremely difficult to take care of. He never went to sleep, would be making all kinds of noise all the time, and twice had actually hid property of the girls.

Bobby Jo could believe it. He was a nasty little guy, so unlike his father, even though he looked a little like him. He had his ears and light blue eyes—the physical traits of Albert—but none of the good stuff.

But he minded his manners around Bobby Jo. She wouldn't stand for crap. She'd crack him in the face as quick as look at him. And he would look at her like he wanted to hit her back, and some days she just hoped he would; then she would give him a lesson he wouldn't soon forget.

Lloyd interrupted her reverie. "You want to dance, babe?"

Bobby Jo wavered. Maybe she could, but if she was late . . . Shit.

"I can't, babe, I got to get home."

"We still got time for a quickie, right?"

Bobby Jo nodded.

On the way home, Bobby Jo wondered what her life would be like if her house burned to the ground. She would make a lot of money. Albert had left her well off, able to live for a long time without working, but she would get all the money for the insurance; Albert had showed her the policy just three weeks before he died.

Little Albert would be gone, and she would be able to start over. She was only nineteen. The idea of having to take care of Albert for years was depressing.

She felt guilty. Sometimes, looking into his eyes, Bobby Jo wanted to cry, she felt so sorry for him. But most of the time he was causing such problems that she didn't like him. It felt good when she could teach him a lesson.

In a way it was too bad she didn't see her father anymore. She didn't know if he was dead or alive—and cared less. But he might be able to take care of Albert.

Anyway, she had made up her mind: she would never see him again.

They pulled into the block where Bobby Jo's house was. All was dark and quiet except for lights in some of the windows of her house.

Lloyd pulled to a stop about a half block from her house and, wordlessly, because they knew the routine by heart, they got into the back seat, disrobed, and fucked.

Bobby Jo, of course, did not come. But she got satisfaction of a sort, and she always liked to see how fast she could make Lloyd come. She had gotten it down to about four minutes.

Tonight it took her four and a half minutes. Then again, Lloyd had been drinking.

Lloyd drove her the rest of the way to her house and let her off. He promised to call her the next day.

"Don't call early," she said. Bobby Jo slept late and often didn't get up, if she had gone out the night before, until four or five in the afternoon.

When she was up, she liked to relax and watch TV,

particularly cartoons. She and Little Albert watched them together.

She had thought, at least in the early days after Albert got killed, that she should make more of an effort to keep the house clean, but she didn't. When she had lived with her mother and father she kept the house spotless.

Now, she had very little interest, and anyway when she did clean up Little Albert would somehow mess it up. It was almost as if he was doing it on purpose.

The house was not a complete pigsty, though, because once every two weeks a nigger lady named Olga came in and cleaned. Bobby Jo always felt better after she left. But she was never able to do it herself anymore.

The babysitter, a girl named Naomi who Bobby Jo realized was sixteen—only a few years younger than she— was waiting just inside the door for her. Naomi looked annoyed. Bobby Jo wasn't late. What was the matter?

"Mrs. Brooks," Naomi said, "Albert was terrible tonight. He wouldn't go to sleep, and he was making all these kind of strange mooing noises—it scared me. And once when I went into the room I couldn't see him, and all of a sudden he jumped out at me from behind the door."

Bobby Jo felt something welling up inside her. "I'm sorry, Naomi," she said, handing her some folded-up bills. "Here's an extra dollar for your trouble."

Naomi said nothing. She took the money and looked past Bobby Jo at the street. Bobby Jo heard the sound of a car. It was Naomi's father.

Naomi put on her sweater and looked at Bobby Jo as she did.

"I'm sorry, Mrs. Brooks," she said, "but I can't babysit for you anymore. It's not worth it."

"I could increase your fee," Bobby Jo said.

Naomi shook her head. "I'm sorry. I don't think so."

Bobby Jo watched her go down the path and get into her father's car. It pulled away, and Bobby Jo realized she had seen the last of Naomi.

The little fuck, she thought. *He's just endless trouble.*

She turned and went across the living room and down a short hall. She peered into Albert's room. It was dark—Albert wanted a night-light but Bobby Jo wouldn't allow it.

She went over to his bed. The blankets were rumpled, but she realized that Albert wasn't there.

"Where are you?" she said tightly.

No answer.

She thought of where he might be and was about to leave the room when she smelled it. A foul smell, like cat crap, but that couldn't be. Six months earlier she had gotten Albert a kitten, but neither of them could control it. It crapped all over the house and stunk up everything. So one day when she was doing a load of laundry Bobby Jo drowned it in the sink, then dried it off, fluffed it up, and showed it to Albert, telling him that the poor thing had somehow just died.

Albert didn't want to give it up. He wanted to keep it in his room with his other toys, and after she had thrown it out she had caught Albert searching through the garbage can.

She knew he felt the loss. She heard him crying every night for a long time.

So, then, what was the smell and where was it coming from?

It was inside the room. Somewhere.

Bobby Jo turned on the ceiling light.

She looked under the bed.

Nothing. Then she glanced at the one closet in the room. The door was closed. She walked toward it, and as she did the smell got stronger.

She opened the closet door and almost gagged. The smell enveloped her.

Albert was sitting in the bottom of the closet clutching a toy, looking down, his face scrunched up, trying to play on her sympathy.

"What are you doing? What did you do?"

Albert said nothing.

"Answer me!" Bobby Jo screamed. "Answer me!"

Albert looked up. He had tears in his eyes. "I was scared."

"Of what? What are you scared of?"

"Noises. Things. Noises and things."

"What did you do? What did you do?"

Bobby Jo felt tears come to her eyes. This little bastard.

She went out of the room and down the hall and into the bathroom. She turned on the hot water full blast.

She stormed back into the room. Albert was still in the closet.

"You shit your pants!" she screamed. "You shit your pants. Can't you ever, ever, ever do anything right? Must you always be like this? Huh? Huh? I have no life because of you. No life at all. And you . . . you took . . . took your father's life. Did you know that? Did you know that!"

"Oh, Mommy, please, please . . ."

Bobby Jo dragged him out of the closet and started to hit him. She hit him wherever her hand fell—face, behind, back . . . Her hand was covered with shit. She didn't care. She wanted to destroy this little bastard . . . bastard . . . bastard . . .

140

Then she dragged him down the hall by one arm.

Outside the bathroom she stopped and stripped his clothing off. "You need a bath, you little bastard. Bad."

Albert became aware of what was about to happen. He started to kick as she wrenched him into the bathroom, which was filled with steam, and pulled him toward the tub.

Bobby Jo's voice became low. She had a distant brief memory of something involving herself and her father, and then she plunged Albert into the scalding water.

His scream did not sound human.

CHAPTER 21

Albert Brooks III was having a dream, and he was terrified.

He was in a small room, and it was completely dark. He could have held his fingers next to his eyes and not have been able to see them.

The thing that scared Albert was that he realized he was not alone—there was something else in the room with him that he couldn't see.

He did not want to see what it was, but he strained his eyes to do just that. Somehow he knew that whatever it was was directly across the room from the corner he was in.

He looked and looked and could see nothing, but occasionally he thought he heard some movement.

Maybe, he thought, *the thing is asleep*.

Albert froze. Suddenly, savagely, a pair of large eyes appeared directly across the room. They were round, yellow eyes with black centers. Owl eyes.

The eyes hated him. You could see the hatred in the eyes.

Albert closed his eyes; maybe this would make him invisible to the thing.

He kept them squeezed closed for what seemed like a long time. He opened them. The eyes were still looking at him, only they seemed to have gotten bigger.

No. They were *closer*.

Albert opened his mouth to scream, but he couldn't. He could not make a sound.

Suddenly, the eyes started to move upward—straight up. But not for a moment did they stop looking at Albert.

Then Albert saw something more. A flash of huge wings. The wings seemed to spread as wide as the door. They moved silently.

He could see more. A beak. He could see the beak on the thing. It was a bird, an owl, only huge.

Albert could see blood dripping from the beak.

The eyes stopped far above, looking down. Albert knew what it was going to do. It was going to get him. Swoop down and get him, like a little thing.

It stared down cruelly at him. It knew it had him. Albert tried to move but couldn't. He was trapped.

He screamed silently into the darkness.

The bird-thing started down, its great wings flapping silently, its bloody red beak opening.

Albert felt a warm sensation in the lower part of his body.

He awoke, terrified, crying, and then realized he was awake, but that didn't help much—another fear clutched at him.

He had wet his pants—again.

Mommy hated that. She had told him before that the

next time she caught him doing that she would ship him out and he would never come back. She didn't want a little pissy-pants around her house. It stunk. It was dirty and embarrassing.

It was just one of so many ways Albert hurt Mommy.

Albert had sworn that he would not do it again.

It was nighttime. Albert got up very carefully out of the bed so it didn't squeak and put his ear next to the wall of the room where Mommy slept.

He listened. He couldn't hear anything like he could when she had friends over; then he could hear her easily.

Maybe she was asleep.

Albert tiptoed to his door, which was partially open, and slipped through into the hall. There was a small light sticking out of the wall.

Slowly and carefully he tiptoed down the hall to his mother's room.

The door was open. He looked in, his eyes gradually getting accustomed to the light.

There was no one there. The bed was empty. Albert breathed a sigh of relief. He was alone in the house.

Quickly he went back to his room and stripped his pajamas off, dropping them on the floor. Then he stripped the sheets off his bed; they stunk.

He rolled them up in a ball and dropped them on top of the pajamas.

He was little, but he knew he could do it. He had to.

He grabbed one side of the mattress and pulled. It was a single bed and not that heavy.

It took him a couple of minutes, but he soon was able to turn it over. He felt it. It was dry.

Still nude, he picked up the sheets and pajamas.

He tried to think where to hide the stuff. It was a big

house and there were plenty of places, but Mommy seemed to know them all.

No, there was one place she hardly ever went. To the cellar. She would send him down there when he was bad, which was a lot, but she hardly ever came down there. There wasn't anything there except the coal bin, a workshop where his daddy used to work, a furnace, and lots of boxes and stuff.

Mommy would always put him in the cellar with the lights off. It might be better if he went down with the lights off. If he had them on and she came home . . .

But he could not bear to go down with the lights off. That's what always scared him, being down there in the dark. There was only one small window, and it was very dirty, so that even in daylight the basement was sort of dark. At night it was black.

His ears were peeled for sounds of Mommy coming home, and sounds from the basement. He turned the light on and then went down the long single flight of wooden steps. A couple creaked, scaring him even more.

At the foot of the stairs he thought about what to do. There were so many places to hide it. But if she ever found out . . .

The furnace roared on, and Albert glanced over at it. He had his solution.

He went to the furnace, a big black iron thing with a coal and fire door. He stood a moment listening to it roar.

He used a metal thing to pull open the fire door. The flames were yellow. He could feel the heat on his entire body.

He balled the sheets and pajamas up as tightly as he could and threw them into the furnace. Then he shut the door.

Smoke billowed out the door, then died down.

Albert was safe. She would never find them.

He went back upstairs, found a clean sheet in the dresser, and put it on the mattress.

He was sweaty. He went into the bathroom and climbed up on a stool so he could see himself in the mirror. He looked dirty.

Quickly, he washed his hands and face and then dried them on the side of the towel facing the wall.

He went back into his room and put on clean pajamas.

He could not sleep. He kept thinking about things, but his mind kept coming back to one thing, a cat he sometimes saw on the block. It had gray and white stripes and was smart.

Albert would have trouble catching it, but he bet he could. And he wondered how far it could run with its belly cut open.

CHAPTER 22

JUNE 6, 1969, 9:00 A.M.

Little Albert was happy, happier than he had been in his whole entire life.

It was because of Mommy. Mommy was being so nice to him. She was not like she usually was, which was mean. No, for the last three days she had been very nice to Albert, even though on all those days he was not a good boy. Every single night he went to the bathroom in bed, like he usually did. When Mommy would beat him for doing it he would promise her that he would never do it again, but he always did. For as long as he could remember he would wake up in the middle of the night, in the darkness, feeling wet and warm. And sometimes worse. Sometimes he poopooed. Once Mommy made him eat it. It tasted terrible.

But Mommy was so nice to him now. She didn't beat him, or make him take baths so hot that his skin would hurt for days afterward.

She said it was all right that he went to the bathroom in bed. She said accidents happened.

Little Albert was also happy because Mommy got up in the morning. Usually she slept very late. Albert had been going to kindergarten now, and on most days he went with Jimmy Briles, a friend who lived two houses away, and Jimmy's mommy.

A couple of times he got a ride from one of his uncles who came to see Mommy and slept over.

But on the last three days Mommy had taken him. Albert was proud. He liked to show he had a mommy like everybody else.

He liked the house better too, because Mommy had cleaned it. For such a long time everything had been all over the place except when the cleaning lady came in, but Mommy had spent the last three days cleaning it.

Albert wondered why Mommy had gotten him dressed up today. It was Saturday. Usually he just got up and watched cartoons on Saturday, and he would stay in his pajamas unless he was a bad boy. Then he would change.

But today she got him all dressed up before he started to watch cartoons. He felt a little funny watching cartoons all dressed up.

"Are you going to get dressed up, Mommy?"

"No," she said.

"Are we going anywhere?"

She shook her head no.

Albert watched a lot of different cartoons until around ten o'clock, when he became aware that someone had come to the front door. It scared him, like a lot of other things scared him.

He heard Mommy talking to the person. It was a deep voice, the voice of a man.

It scared Albert.

The voices got louder, and Mommy came into the room with the person. Albert, who was sitting on the floor, looked up.

It was a very old man and very big. He was smiling at Albert, and so was Mommy. Albert smiled back, though he didn't like people looking at him like Mommy and the man were.

"This is Mr. Kennedy," Mommy said.

Mr. Kennedy smiled and bent over. He put out his hand and shook Albert's hand. Albert stood up.

"How are you, lad," he said. "You're a fine-looking boy. Glad to meet you."

Mommy looked at Albert. "Today," she said, "you are going to go to Mr. Kennedy's house for a visit."

The idea scared Albert, but he said nothing.

"You'll be staying there a while," she said, "but I'll be coming to visit you."

The word popped out of Albert's mouth before he could stop it: "Where?"

"Albany," she said. "That's a nice city upstate."

Albert nodded.

Ten minutes later, Albert was ready to go. Mommy had packed a suitcase for him, and she walked out of the house with Mr. Kennedy and him. Albert was very scared.

They stopped at a big black car parked at the curb, and Mr. Kennedy opened the front door for Albert.

Albert looked up at Mommy. She knelt down. She had tears in her eyes, and suddenly Albert was very, very scared and he felt like crying.

She hugged him. "I'll visit you, little Albert," she said. "Everything will be fine."

Albert's lower lip curled down and he got tears in his eyes. He said nothing.

"Go in the car now," Mommy said.

Albert got in the car. It was very big and had a funny smell.

The man closed the door and went around and got into the driver's seat. He smiled at Albert as he did.

Albert turned and looked at Mommy. She was standing there with her arms folded in front of her, and then she reached up and wiped a tear away.

Tears started to blur Albert's eyes.

Mommy, he wanted to say. *Mommy!* But he said nothing.

The car started to move down the street. Albert turned and kept Mommy in sight as long as he could.

She waved, and kept waving. The last thing Albert saw when the big car made a turn was the top of the house.

"How you doin', lad?" the man said.

Albert just looked at him.

It took him a month before he found out that he was now something known as a foster child, and that he would be living with the Kennedys indefinitely.

As it happened, Mommy came to visit him once, and then he never saw her again for the rest of his life.

But that was okay, because he had come to realize something long before that: He didn't give a fuck.

CHAPTER 23

Benton left the Bronx for the drive down to see Jim Brosnan at around two in the morning.

He was looking forward to the trip.

For one thing, there was the case. When he was finished looking at what Jim had he would know a lot more about just who the killer was.

There would also be the simple joy of wallowing in the details of eleven gory murders—what more could a body ask?

And another thing. He would be basking in the glory of an earlier day. Four years before, Benton had been picked by the NYPD to attend a special homicide school—cops who attended nicknamed it the University of Homicide at Quantico—and Benton did very well. Indeed, there was an unstated but widely held belief that Benton was one of the best students the academy had ever had, and the cops who went there represented the best from homicide units all over the country—and some foreign countries.

He would never forget what Brosnan had said to him

one martini-littered night: "If you were a killer, George, we would be in deep shit."

Of course there was no telling how he would react to remembering the time he spent there with Joyce. It was the last good time he had with her. The deterioration in their relationship really started after he got out of the academy.

They had some wonderful times, though.

They lived in an apartment in Quantico, and every chance they got they would take long wonderful drives through the mountains of Virginia, take in the sights in Washington, and make trips into the south, where they were fascinated by the tough, gnarled, life-scarred faces of the men who worked the mines and the women who waited at home.

It was a time when there were still stars in her eyes, when George Benton was still someone special.

Still, he knew he would be okay. He just knew it.

He crossed into Virginia at dawn feeling only semi-lonely—wonderful!—and stopped for a Perrier and an unbuttered bran muffin at a diner just outside Quantico. Then he drove to the Marine base where the FBI academy was located.

He was questioned briefly by a crew-cut, ramrod-straight Marine—they never changed, he thought—and then drove onto the base.

As he drove up the road toward the administration building, he could see that things there had changed—dramatically. It seemed that they had been building nonstop since he left, because there were at least five new buildings and construction in progress on three or four more. Everywhere the earth was turned over, and everywhere there was heavy machinery.

Crime, he thought, *the ultimate employer.*

Benton got to the administration building at around a quarter to eight. He identified himself to the person behind the counter, signed in, and was given a pass to wear.

A call was made, and he was told that Jim would be there to meet him shortly.

Five minutes later, Jim Brosnan came through a hall adjacent to the reception area. He was a thin—painfully thin—guy who wore prescription sunglasses. He had a sad face that was not at all expressive of his personality; he was quite upbeat.

He had always appalled Benton a bit. He smoked at least two and a half packs a day of those thin, loathsome little cigars—which he inhaled—and he always used extra salt and butter on his food. He also drank about twenty cups of coffee a day.

On the other hand, Benton thought, he was an ecto-morph, almost a skeleton, and would probably last for-ever. At ninety he would still be sipping coffee and inhaling cigarillos, gazing at the world through a milky, cataract-scarred eyes, and Benton would be history.

Jim took off his glasses. He had soft brown eyes. He shook Benton's hand. "Good to see you, George. Real good."

"You too, Jim," Benton said, feeling a deep warmth inside.

"Want some breakfast?" Jim asked. "No, right?"

"No, yes," Benton said, laughing.

Benton followed Brosnan through a maze of halls. Dur-ing the months that Benton had been there he had never been able to figure them out exactly.

He liked being with Jim. It somehow filled up some empty place inside him.

"How's the NYPD?"

"Not what it used to be."

"So I hear."

"Over seventy percent of the people have less than five years' experience, and the quality definitely isn't what it once was."

"What goes around comes around," Brosnan said.

"Believe it."

Brosnan led Benton to an elevator and they went down two floors to the basement—"No one's lower than us," Brosnan said, spouting his standard line.

The basement consisted of another maze of offices, conference rooms, computer rooms, occupied by people— from agents to secretaries—who in one way or another were involved in the never-ending war on violent crime.

Brosnan paused in front of one of the doors. "Sure you don't have time for coffee?"

"Only homicide," Benton said.

Brosnan opened the door and then went inside. It was a large conference room dominated by a long wooden table. There was a phone at one end and, at the other, two thick piles of documents.

"These are the files," Brosnan said, stepping over to them. "Ten in all."

"You should get two duplicates of number eleven in a couple of days."

"Good."

Benton stepped over and looked at the files. For a moment Jim Brosnan ceased to exist. Benton was totally absorbed by the files, completely projected into them, excited, appalled, thrilled.

Each represented, in a sense, a life and the end of a life, a young life.

Now, here, it was up to Benton to try to unravel some

of the answers, to get a better sense of who this killer was. And fast. Each moment lost could be precious. He was not dramatizing it. There it was, a twist on what Heirens had said: Stop him before he kills more.

"If you need anything," Brosnan said, "you can reach me on extension 3298. Maps are on the shelf at the far end of the room."

Benton nodded.

Brosnan moved toward the doorway, stopped, and turned. "You better break for lunch," he said, "and you better have dinner with my wife and me—or you're a dead man."

Benton smiled. Brosnan was a little weird, like him.

Brosnan left, closing the door behind him.

The files had tabs on the edge with the victim's name and the date of her death. Referring to the tabs, Benton laid the files out, one next to the other, in a line along the table starting from the first to the most recent.

He sat down in front of the first folder and opened it up.

He read the police report, then the autopsy, then the lab results.

The victim's name was Julia Schmitt. She was blond and weighted between 108 and 110 and was anywhere from five two to five four; estimates were necessary because she was, like all the other victims, headless; the ME had made the calculation based on a human head being one-eighth to one-tenth of the body weight; height had been calculated based on overall physiognomy.

She had been a student at Monmouth College in Long Branch, New Jersey.

Benton had a pretty good idea where it was. Down on the south shore of Jersey. He got up and went to a shelf where the maps were and leafed through them until he came across one that included south Jersey. He found Long Branch easily, down on the south shore.

He had heard of Monmouth College. It was a ritzy place, having once been somebody's private estate.

The body had been found by the railroad station, about fifty yards down the tracks.

Benton selected one of the pictures showing the victim in the morgue, washed off, all wounds showing.

A motorman had found the body. In fact, he thought he had run the girl down, particularly since she was headless.

But that was all, really. Compared to the last victim, she was relatively unscathed, but was arranged in the same fetal position as the latest victim, Michelle Reynolds.

Benton leafed through the 8 x 10 color photos taken at the scene and in the morgue. Then he stood up and proceeded to open all the files in turn and look through the photos until he came to the one from each group that he wanted—namely, a shot of each victim washed so the full extent of wounds could be seen.

Then he put them all together and slowly leafed through them. The bodies all had two things in common: they were headless and had been arranged in a fetal position. But they were all different, and when he looked at them five or six times, he could see the pattern that he had suspected. The killer was getting more and more ferocious.

You could almost plot the mutilation on a graph. The first body was headless, the second was headless and badly bruised, the third had a breast removed, the fourth had a breast removed and the vaginal vault stabbed numerous times, the fifth a breast removed and the vagina very badly cut, as if the killer was getting ready for the excision.

The sixth had deep cuts in the vagina, a breast removed, and the other breast stabbed. The seventh and eighth were about the same. The ninth was where both breasts were amputated, and the sheer ferocity of the killer seemed to escalate. The tenth victim had the full catastrophe, and so did the eleventh—Michelle Reynolds.

It was, Benton thought, the classic lustmurderer pattern.

He thought of Jack the Ripper, the classic of classics. He had five victims, all done over a forty-day period. His first victim was comparatively sedately done; the last, Annie Chapman, was found with her intestines hanging off a dresser and her liver by her left foot.

That's the way most serial killers were.

Benton thought of Gacy. He started by assaulting kids sexually, and his games got rougher and rougher until, finally, he killed.

That's the way Armstrong was, and Bundy, and Brudos, and so many others.

Why?

He didn't know, not specifically, but, from all the psychological literature he had read on the subject, he had a certain sense that the killer was working out problems in his own head, problems that required more and more radical solutions, more and more ferocious attention.

Benton put the photos back in their respective folders.

He examined the dates and times the victims were killed.

January 1 was the first. Happy New Year.

Then February 13, March 10, April 7, May 1, June 2, July 5, August 5, September 10, October 30, November 2. Benton looked at the dates for a long time. There was no pattern, except that they were monthly—and getting closer together. Maybe. September 10, October 30, November 2 . . . Close.

He thought about the Schmitt girl.

What were the chances of her becoming a victim? She

was a student, lived in an apartment off campus. Benton didn't know the neighborhood, but it probably wasn't that bad.

Students were good prey, though. It would be easy for a killer to walk onto a campus—particularly a young killer—and pick out a victim and stalk her until the time was right.

That's what Bundy did a few times, and Armstrong, and a couple of others. You could not only go unnoticed, but there were enough types so you could look for whatever it was you needed before you killed.

Symbols, criteria, Benton thought, all these killers had them, inner tests that the victim knew nothing about. Failing meant life; passing death.

Benton remembered Hanson in Anchorage, his criteria. He had abducted over forty girls, killing seventeen by flying them to a remote island, releasing them nude, and then hunting them down with a long gun.

He had three criteria: First the girl had to approach him sexually. Second, he had to offer to do something to her sexually that she found repulsive. And third, she had to try to escape.

That's what tripped him up. A fourteen-year-old prostitute had satisfied the first two criteria, but she didn't try to escape, so he told investigators, "I had to let her go."

She went, right to the cops.

Benton went back to the first victim.

She had last been seen about four o'clock on the day she was first discovered missing.

The last person to see her alive was a friend named Dolores Wolfe. They had a late lunch, then spent the afternoon together. She left Dolores's house at around five o'clock and drove home. Wolfe said she had seen Schmitt get into her car and drive away.

She never got to the house on Johnson Street where she had a room. The landlady said that she was around the house at about the time the Schmitt girl should have returned home but didn't.

Her car, a 1982 blue Honda Civic, was never found.

The coroner said she was killed elsewhere. There was virtually no blood in her body.

The second victim, Daphne Tedesco, lived with her parents in Newark. She was also blond, about five five, 120 pounds.

Benton looked at what appeared to be a high school graduation picture of the girl. Blond, pretty.

He got up and went to each of the folders, in turn looking for and finding a candid shot of the victim. He found nine and laid them side by side on the table. Some were pretty, some ordinary-looking, but it appeared that he had found the link: the hair. Every single one was blond.

He replaced the pictures and sat down again.

He read about the second victim: She worked five days a week at Prudential, where she was a secretary. She lived with her parents and drove to and from work. She was last seen alive at work. Co-workers said she left at the normal time, five o'clock. They assumed she went to her car, which was in a lot down the street.

The car was found, abandoned, in the South Side section of Newark.

The crime scene report on the car was negative: not a drop of blood, a hair, or prints, except latents that belonged to the victim, and others that were too smeared to be of any value.

Benton stared at the crime scene report. He wondered about its quality. He had a dim view, generally, of the work of crime scene units and labs: they were inexperienced, understaffed, underpaid, undermotivated. More than occasionally Benton would find himself second-guessing results.

The third victim's name was Joan Seaman, and she was a commercial artist in Morristown, New Jersey, with the PAT Data Communications Company.

She was twenty-three, but estimated to be only five feet one inch—shorter than the other victims.

She had been killed on March 10, which was a Tuesday. Another artist with the company told an investigator that she had left work about five.

She also had a car. It was discovered, abandoned, in a shopping mall in Parsippany, which apparently was only ten or fifteen minutes from Morristown.

The car, a 1979 Buick Le Sabre, was clean of any evidence; there were no prints except the victim's.

On April 7, victim number four: Jo Anne Miller, age twenty, she also drove a car, and Benton made another link: all the victims drove cars.

Her body was found in a construction shack off Route 287.

She worked in a delicatessen in Morristown. She had closed the store at ten o'clock—her boss was there with her—and left for home, which was an apartment she shared with a boyfriend.

She never got there. Her body was found behind the Chase Rabbinical School just outside of town, just off the road in some weeds. Her car, a Ford Lynx, had not been found.

Another insight, not unexpected: All of the victims, thus far, were easy to find.

The fifth victim's name was Rosalinde Berne. She worked

160

as a computer technician for AT&T in Holmdel, New Jersey.

She was tall and thin—five feet nine but only 115 pounds. At twenty-six she was older than the others.

The case was different, too, in that all the victims up to her did not arrive home. She did. She lived with her parents in Lincroft, New Jersey.

Benton referred to the map showing Holmdel. Lincroft was not far away.

He went down the police report. Her parents said that she went out about eight o'clock and never came back.

Her body was discovered on a dirt road about three miles from the AT&T building. Her car, a 1983 gray Chevy Impala, was found a hundred yards away, and again, there was nothing in the car that could be remotely related to the killer.

Indeed, Benton thought, there was nothing anywhere that could be related to the killer.

He was about to go through the file of the sixth victim when he was startled by Jim Brosnan poking his head in the door.

"How you doin', George?"

"Okay."

"How about some lunch?"

"I'm okay."

Brosnan eyed him. "Okay," he said. "But before you leave Washington I do demand your presence at my house for dinner."

"Absolutely."

Brosnan smiled and closed the door.

Benton opened the file on victim number six. It was a non-Jersey victim. Her name was Anne Jacobs, and she

161

lived on Victory Boulevard in Staten Island with two other girls.

She was twenty years old, five three, weighed about 120 pounds. She had been a student at the College of Staten Island, and that was the last place she had been seen alive.

"She worked in the school library until around nine," one of her roommates said, "and that night she just didn't come home."

The woman's supervisor at the library said that the victim had been working right up until closing time. "In fact," the supervisor added, "I saw her walking down the path toward the parking lot. I saw her under the streetlight, and then she was gone."

Her body was discovered on a dirt side road off Route 440 near the Fresh Kills dump. Her car was found on Route 9 in Old Bridge, New Jersey.

Again, no evidence was found in her car, a 1985 Toyota Celica.

The seventh victim, Mary Beth Gorman, lived in Old Bridge, New Jersey, but that's where any connection to the other victims ended. She had been a go-go dancer in a club, the Electric Pussy Cat, in Old Bridge.

She was five seven, twenty-four, and was estimated to have weighed 135 pounds.

Her body was found behind Westwood, a private school, not far outside Old Bridge. There was no car, and the police report said she had no car. The FBI had a course on what they termed "victimology"—a go-go dancer would be at higher risk of being a victim than the others, who were low risk.

It was outside the pattern.

Just exactly when she disappeared was hazy. The first time anyone realized she was missing was July 6, when the woman who watched her two-year-old boy reported to the police that she had not returned the previous night.

The manager of the Electric Pussy Cat had no idea what had happened to her, and in the brief comments that were in the police report—like "who knows about these broads" —you could tell he couldn't care less.

One of the cops had spoken to another dancer at the club, and she remembered Mary Beth talking to a couple of guys at the bar between sets, but she didn't see her leave with anyone. The other dancer had left before Mary Beth.

Sometimes, Benton thought, serial murderers worked in pairs—Otis Toole and Henry Lee Lucus were the two who sprang to mind—but it was usually a solo activity. Just a lone killer and his victims.

The eighth victim was within the pattern of the others. She worked as a secretary in a data processing firm in Parsippany, New Jersey.

Benton recalled that one of the victims had worked in Morristown but lived in Parsippany. Not that it meant anything, but there it was.

The victim's name was Anne Langford. She had been reported missing on August 5, when she didn't return from a movie she had seen with her boyfriend. She had dropped him off at his house, then had driven home.

Her body was discovered in an abandoned construction site a few miles out of town.

Abandoned, Benton thought, but still near enough to a road that her body was bound to be discovered.

Her car, a Ford station wagon, was found nearby.

The mutilation escalated with victim nine, one Adrienne Lowell.

Benton looked at the candid of her. She was at the

beach, in a bathing suit, standing near a step railing, smiling.

She had a nice figure, big breasts.

Benton realized what Barbara Babalino had suggested: maybe he was picking victims by their chest size. That, he thought, wasn't true. In fact it was probably meaningless to the killer. The detail was the hair, her blond hair shining in the sun.

But the killer had taken off her breasts. There was, he thought, something so obscene about it.

A memory, Bundy again. He was so good at what he did. Benton remembered Brosnan saying that of all the serial murderers he had ever encountered, Bundy had garnered the most respect.

"He was slick," Brosnan had said once at a local watering hole. "Christ, the day he came to Sammashish State Park looking for someone to kill he had one arm in a phony sling and was asking girls to help him pick up his boat. He was good-looking and articulate. He was bound to catch anyone except the most wary. That guy could have caught a policewoman."

Benton couldn't disagree. Not many people walked around expecting to be conned by a serial killer.

The Lowell woman worked in Clifton, where she was a secretary in a publishing company. Her body had been found, the police report stated, in an abandoned building just a few blocks from her employer, Clifton Press. She had a car, but it had not been recovered.

Benton came to the last case before Michelle Reynolds.

Her name was Darlene Santora. She was five eight, maybe 140, big.

Benton was struck by something instantly. Darlene Santora worked for AT&T in Freehold; another victim also did.

He went back to the fifth folder and looked at it. Yes. Rosalinde Berne. She worked for AT&T in Holmdel.

Was there a connection? AT&T was a big company, it had thousands of employees. But two victims from there? It strained credibility, right? Then again, that's the way homicide investigations were. Filled with unlikely happenings. For the moment, he would let it sit.

Benton took a break, a short walk down one of the corridors to a water fountain. He took a drink, stretched, went back inside.

So much for lunch.

He sat back down and started going through the files again. *Ho-ho*, he thought. *The first thousand fucking times you go through them are the hardest!*

He was going through the file of Mary Beth Gorman, the seventh victim, when he realized something, and he carefully went through all of the autopsy reports to confirm it.

Estimating time of death was an iffy proposition, far more imprecise than people believed. But it would seem that only Michelle Reynolds had been found within a few—actually four—hours of death. All the others were in various advanced states of death, as it were. They were dead a minimum ten to thirty-six hours before discovery and their bodies had been held somewhere else before being dumped.

Of course you might suppose the bodies were dumped quickly and then they deteriorated until the moment of discovery. But logic was against that. Somebody would have discovered at least one of the bodies earlier. Christ, the first victim was found near the railroad station, another on Route 440, another off Route 287— not exactly the Okefenokee Swamp.

No, if the bodies were there to see, someone would have seen them.

They simply weren't there.

The question, then, assuming his theory was correct, was why. Why would the killer dump the body of Michelle Reynolds so soon after death—and not the others?

He did not know.

Benton worked his way through the other files and then did it again. The idea was to make all the details of all the cases instantly accessible.

"This procedure can"—as one old-time homicide sergeant once said—"lead to good things."

Good things being connections and patterns.

He briefly debated with himself whether to go through the material a fourth time, then decided against it.

It was eight o'clock. He had been up since midnight, and though he didn't feel tired, he might be. He could miss something, and he didn't want to take that chance. He arranged the files in two piles and left the conference room.

He was able to find his way out after only three wrong turns.

He turned in his badge, then walked down lawn-flanked paths to the parking lot where his car was.

It was dark and cold with a light rain falling.

The sky was very dark, but still he could see construction machines silhouetted against it, like some kind of prehistoric monsters.

He shuddered, and not just from the cold. He had a sense of unease.

There were only a few cars in the parking lot. His car, which was wedged in among others when he had parked, was alone.

He was almost to it when he stopped. A connection, just like that, made his hair stand up a little: Every single one of the victims had been abducted in the dark. And killed. Snatched and killed in the darkness.

He started walking again. His mind scanned the file material.

Even the victims, he thought, who were abducted when daylight saving time was in effect were grabbed in the dark. The killer had to wait until it was dark.

It was, he thought, the best time to do it. Darkness and death were friends.

He got into his car and sat there, the light rain pattering down on the windshield, and thought: Bundy operated in daylight—and night. Kemper in daylight. The Yorkshire Ripper at night, Jack the Ripper at night. Gacy at night, Gein in daylight and at night, Fish daylight and night, Dean Corrl at night, Armstrong in daylight.

It was not significant, at least in terms of the MO. What it meant to the killer was something else.

He turned the car on, let it warm up for a minute, and drove out of the parking lot.

The last thing he saw before he exited the base was the image in his rearview mirror of the construction machinery.

He could swear it was about to move.

Crazy, he thought, and smiled in the darkness of his car. He better get some sleep.

CHAPTER 24

In his motel room Benton was up until 2:00 A.M. thinking about the case, but by seven the next morning he was sitting in the same diner he had eaten in the day before.

This time he figured he needed to eat something substantial. Bran muffins and Perrier would not keep him going indefinitely, and this case, he sensed, was going to take some effort.

So he ate a couple of eggs and dry toast and quaffed two cups of coffee.

It felt good just eating and drinking all that shit. Let the devil take tomorrow!

He was back at the academy at eight.

Jim escorted him in again. "How'd you do, George?"

"I think well. But you never know." Benton told him about the insights he had had.

"Sounds good to me," Brosnan said. "On the money."

Then Benton told Brosnan about the time-of-death discrepancy. "What do you make of it?"

"Maybe they were abducted, taken to a remote location, done, then driven back and dumped."

"That's a possibility," Benton said. "Which could mean that the murder site is close to the Bronx.

"Or maybe in it. All the dump sites were pretty good, but the Bronx site was perfect. He really had to know the Bronx well."

Benton nodded and said nothing. There was no way to prove that Jim was right. There were still too many variables.

But Jim himself was a constant. This was his hunch based on mind and heart and experience; it was something Benton would assume true until proven wrong.

At the door to the conference room Brosnan said, "You got my address?"

Benton nodded.

"Tonight at seven show up—or break out your taxes for the last quarter century."

"I'll be there."

Then Benton was alone with the files again.

He went through them very slowly, not only trying to memorize, but to live the details, to imaginatively project himself into murder scenarios so they become as real as possible for him.

It wasn't that difficult. He had been to literally hundreds of autopsies, investigated hundreds of murders, so he could draw on this experience to make the scenes real. He knew how bodies smelled, how they felt, he knew how resistant flesh was to a sharp instrument. He could begin to understand the psychological and physical duress a victim experienced.

What was difficult, and what he wanted to understand better than anything, was what the killer thought and felt before, during, and after a killing.

That was not so easy, he thought, even for him , ho-ho, the Bent One. No matter how many murders you experience, it is still difficult, since you are not a killer, to understand it.

Killers, serial killers, were extraordinarily outside the experience of murder; they cared nothing about the victim. Nothing for the suffering, the agony, the terror.

Benton remembered that neighbors said that they used to hear screaming and crying coming from the direction of John Gacy's house in the middle of the night. Gacy was torturing his victims, sodomizing them with a huge dildo, choking them, playing with their minds and hearts so that they didn't know from one minute to the next whether they were going to live or die.

But Gacy didn't care. He killed thirty-three young boys and didn't care at all.

Kemper seemingly cared, or at least paid lip service to the idea that he did. But Kemper didn't care. How could you care if you killed? The concepts were in diametric opposition.

Benton smiled. Diametric opposition. Wouldn't the boys in the squad room love to hear that kind of language.

Bundy didn't care, Fish didn't care, none of them cared. At least in terms of how the victims felt. They felt nothing at all.

So, then, what did they feel?

Benton looked at the pictures of Michelle Reynolds. What was left of her.

What was the killer feeling when he was doing her?

Benton closed his eyes. He imagined himself on top of Michelle Reynolds, biting her hard enough to draw blood, then taking the time to use a sharp instrument to cut off each of her breasts, and then to carve out her vaginal vault.

Rage. That had to be one thing. Rage against her, or what she represented.

Not just rage. White-hot rage.

Anything else?

Had to be. Look at the MO. Cutting up a body, getting off that. Sexual pleasure. Lustmurderers got sexual pleasure out of cutting the victim.

Why?

In a sense, he thought, it had to be some positive action on the part of the killer. It accomplished something beyond rage.

Benton froze.

Control. That's what it was. Control. The killer dominated the body, controlled it.

He looked at one of the 8 x 10's of Michelle Reynolds at the scene.

He had canceled out her very humanity, destroying her sex organs and taking off her head.

Why? Why that way? Why not just kill her? Wouldn't that do the same thing?

He closed his eyes and put his head back. He thought about it for a long time but couldn't crack it.

Forget that, Benton thought, why would he kill these people in one place and dump them in another?

Why did he want them found?

To challenge. Challenge who? The cops. Yes, authority, definitely. Showing up at cop watering holes was the same thing. A challenge.

Did he know the places where he dumped the bodies? Did he live in the areas?

No. No one could live in all those areas.

Why not? A traveling salesman could have lived in all

those places. Researched them as good spots to dump bodies, but not so good that they wouldn't be found.

You couldn't assume he lived in the areas permanently. But you had to assume he had lived there for a while. No one could come up with dump places like the ones used based on casual contact.

So look for an itinerant—and if Jim's hunch is right, one who was based in the Bronx.

Benton got up and went down to the water cooler, had a drink, and came back.

So, then, putting it all together, what can we surmise?

The suspect is a white male between twenty and thirty; he is stewing inside, and his need to murder—to control?—is getting more ferocious.

He is an itinerant, possibly based in the Bronx.

Blond-haired women are poison to him, symbols of something terrible.

He operates in the darkness, and in all except one case the victim had a car.

A car.

That had to be part of his MO. He would get in the victim's car and then force them to drive somewhere.

Maybe he would talk his way in.

Or jumped in when she stopped at a light.

Or abduct the victim where the car was parked, force her into her car, and then force her to drive somewhere else—to the murder site.

Darkness. He operates in the dark.

What did that mean?

Benton didn't know. Yet.

At around three in the afternoon he stopped perusing the files long enough to call the Five Three.

Barbara Babalino was in the squad room.

"Anything new?" he asked.

"Not yet. We're still doing busywork. Joe didn't get anything from BCI. How about you?"

Benton detailed what had come across. The more brains on it, the better; the more details the brains had, the better the job they could do. It took him ten minutes to lay it all out.

"That's a lot, George," Barbara said.

"But still mostly speculation."

"Sounds good to me."

"Let it be, huh?"

"Yes. So what are you going to do now?"

"I don't know," Benton said. And he didn't. He always tried to let an investigation lead him. "But I don't think I'll be back for a couple of days."

"Good luck, George," Barbara said.

Benton went back to the files, this time focusing on the areas where the victims had been last seen.

There was nothing revelatory he could spot. Just that in all cases the bodies were discovered within three miles of where the victims were last seen alive.

He also looked at the relationship of the places to one another: Holmdel, Freehold, Parsippany, Morristown, Staten Island . . . he saw nothing significant.

After another two treks through the files, Benton Xeroxed the police reports on each of the cases as well as photos of each of the victims at the scene.

Then he left. He figured he would go back to the motel to freshen up—he would change his clothes completely, as he did once every day anyway—and then go to Jim's house.

It was dark outside, and again his car was one of the few in the parking lot.

He approached the car, which was completely dark inside, and stood a moment.

He unlocked the driver's-side door, and the interior light went on.

He glanced into the back of the car, down to the floor, before he sat down behind the wheel.

Something . . .

Nothing.

CHAPTER 25

Jim lived in a pleasant Colonial-style house in a suburb of Washington. It was the kind of place Benton had thought he would share with Joyce one day, and for just a moment he felt a certain emptiness, a sense of unfulfillment.

But the feeling passed; by the time he was ushered into the house by Jim and his attractive blond wife, Rita, he had forgotten about it.

George ate, for him, like a pig. Jim's wife had somehow remembered that he didn't eat much red meat, so she served a delicious sole with lemon dressing that George devoured with a minimum of guilt. It beat bran muffins and Perrier hands down.

After dinner they sat around the living room sipping white wine and talking, naturally, about the case. Rita, an ex-policewoman, was an enthusiastic contributor.

George laid out all he had determined about this Henry the Eighth, and what he had concluded so far. He felt confident about his conclusions, but he was happy when both Jim and Rita agreed with him; it all seemed to hang together pretty well.

"There was one other thing I didn't mention to you about this time-of-death thing," Jim said. "We've found out that serial killers love to drive. Just drive and drive and drive. Maybe this guy's doing that. Just pick 'em up and drive around after killing them.

"But you don't think so," Benton said.

"Not really. It would tie into the profile in terms of running a risk of being caught. But there's one thing that militates against it."

"What's that?"

"We've never come across a serial killer who's done it. Driving endless miles is part of the profile, but not driving those miles with a body on board." He paused. "I do think what I said before holds true: this guy knows the Bronx best. I'd bet he's operating out of there."

No one said anything for a moment, then Rita spoke. "You know, I used to travel from the city to Old Bridge, and I always took the Staten Island Expressway. You go from there down 440 south and then across the Outerbridge Crossing into Jersey. That leads you right to Old Bridge and Freehold, and if you stay on the Garden State Parkway you could go to Holmdel—it's right off the parkway."

"Really," Benton said.

"But more than that," she said, "you know what's clearly visible from the Staten Island Expressway?"

Neither man knew.

"That Staten Island college. It's right there, big as life. A killer traveling the expressway couldn't miss it."

"And perhaps get some ideas?" Jim said.

"Right," Rita said. "And at night, as I remember it, 440 was very dark, deserted. It wouldn't be hard to dump a body there and get away with it.

Near the tail end of the night Jim spoke of his favorite

project: a book he was writing on autoerotic death. He told Benton that there were probably more than a thousand autoerotic deaths a year.

"That's what I like about you, Jim," Benton said. "You know what will hold my interest."

Benton thanked Jim and Rita for the dinner and conversation, and promised to keep them informed on his case.

"If you want a formal profile done, just holler," Jim said, "but I don't think you need one."

Benton left Jim's house at around eleven o'clock, and was driving for about fifteen minutes when he realized he was thirsty. He smiled. It did not necessarily mean he had diabetes miletus. He could just be fucking thirsty.

He wondered where he could get a drink, and was in luck. Looming up on the left of the semi-busy road he was on was a 7-Eleven.

Made sense, he thought, that 7-Eleven's were open all night. If they weren't, what else would there be to heist?

Not uncharacteristically, the 7-Eleven was fairly crowded. It was mostly young people, but there were two oldsters, septuagenarian or even octogenerian. They were both buying beer, and the idea depressed Benton a little. What could your life be like when you were old and you were buying beer at close to eleven o'clock at night? Not too swift.

Young people, he thought, were also buying beer, and he had an insight: They were probably buying it for the same reason as the oldsters—to calm their nerves. Anxiety didn't care how old you were.

As the line moved forward Benton became more aware of the person directly in front of him: a young girl, maybe nineteen. She had long wavy blond hair and wore tight jeans and a dungaree jacket. When she turned Benton saw that she was pretty; she didn't have any makeup on except for a little lipstick. She smelled good.

She glanced at Benton, and the sight of him held her for a moment; perhaps, he thought she thought, this guy was once good-looking.

Or maybe she was thinking, Hey, this guy is older but good-looking. Maybe he wants to get it on?

Sure, Benton thought, *and then what would I do?*

She bought a custard cone and left.

As Benton paid for his drink, he watched through the plate glass as the girl got into a big old battered car—it looked like an Impala—and drove away.

He went outside in enough time to notice which way she went. The opposite direction from where he was going. He got in his car and pulled out.

Benton sipped a diet soda as he drove. Yes, the girl had gone in the opposite direction, and he knew he would never see her again as long as they lived.

As long as she lived.

Then it came again, the feeling that he rarely allowed himself the luxury of. It filled the car and made him feel dangerous.

Anger.

Fragments of images . . .

He remembered his father and mother. All the days, the months, the years that he was left with babysitters while they went out to one social function or another.

He told himself he understood, but he knew also that it scared him no matter who the babysitter was; it scared and angered him.

But, of course, he never said anything. He was too little to say anything; if he did, there were consequences. Terrible consequences, though he had no idea what they were.

He remembered something Dr. Stern had said to him: "Anger is a difficult emotion for most people. They are afraid to express it. They fear the consequences."

Whatever they were.

Benton thought of the blond girl.

It was the right time now, and she could very well be a victim. She was young, blond, it was dark, she was alone, in a car. The perfect victim profile.

His mind swept across the photos of the victims. They didn't have a chance. None of them had a chance. Not against an organized social lustmurderer. He has the advantage because they are prey—and don't know it.

For a moment the images coalesced and Benton saw just one image: the blonde in the 7-Eleven, innocently driving along, licking her cone, and someone stalking her.

He thought of their eyes. The eyes of the dead. Open, staring fixed and dilated, not alive. Eyes that would never look on life again.

He wondered if the victims suffered. Probably not. Lustmurderers would kill fairly quickly, then go to work. That's what the profile told us, right?

But they would suffer because they were denied life. Denied life by some sick fuck who would continue to do it unless stopped.

Benton had to stop him.

CHAPTER 26

At four in the morning, Benton decided to go to Freehold, the town where the next-to-last abduction—the AT&T text processor named Santora—had occurred.

He got some sleep and started out from Quantico about nine o'clock. He reached Freehold, New Jersey, at about one in the afternoon.

He stopped in what seemed like the center of town for directions, then followed a circuitous path to Route 9, the heavily traveled commercialized road on which the AT&T facilities were located.

The AT&T building was one story, a low flat brick job with white escarpment and tall mirrored windows. Not particularly modern, but not as old as some of the buildings Benton had seen near the center of town.

He entered the lobby and went up to a long desk behind which was a switchboard operator with a console and, eyeing him carefully as he approached, a bespectacled guard who seemed much too large for his uniform.

Benton had a fantasy of the guy beating on him with a pipe, but instead the guard said, "May I help you?"

Benton showed him his tin. "My name is George Benton. I'm with the NYPD, and I'm here to look into the case that may be related to one we have."

"What's that?"

"Darlene Santora," Benton said.

"I'll call the chief of security," the guard said.

A minute later the chief of security, a bald, trim man in his mid-fifties, emerged from one of the two halls flanking the reception desk. He eyed Benton carefully as he came.

"I'm John Sheehan. May I help?"

"George Benton." He showed his tin again.

"Why don't we go into my office. Bob, will you give Mr. Benton a visitor's pass."

The guard made out a pass and slipped it into a plastic holder that Benton clipped to the collar of the overcoat he was wearing.

It only took Benton a few minutes to establish his authenticity; it helped that Sheehan had been "on the job" in Asbury Heights.

"You have multiple entrances here, right?"

"Three public entrances."

"All guarded?"

"Yeah."

"How effective is it?"

"We keep out the casual intruder. I guess someone could get in if they tried hard enough."

"Do you know anything about the Santora homicide."

"Not really. It was established by Freehold detectives that she was killed outside the building."

"How did they do that?"

Sheehan held his hands out. "I don't know."

"Would it be possible," Benton said, "to see the area where she worked? Also, I'd like to talk with anyone who worked with her."

"Sure. I can show you where her office was and introduce you to her supervisor, Valerie Perry."

"That's great."

Benton and the security chief walked down a long carpeted corridor; every now and then, to his left and right, were other corridors with offices in them.

At one point, Sheehan made a right turn down one of the corridors, and he and Benton had to go carefully: There were some workmen, and the tools and materials of their trade, which appeared to be installing ceiling tile, were lying around the floor.

They walked down another long hall where there were more workmen, and then Sheehan led Benton into a large room where there were four or five computers set up; two of them were being used by young women, one black and young, the other white and in her early thirties.

Benton followed Sheehan over to the white woman. She was slim and dark-haired, with cheerful dark eyes and freckles.

"This is Valerie Perry," he said. "George Benton, a detective from New York City. He wanted to ask some questions about Darlene."

Valerie got up and shook his hand. A shadow had passed across her face when Darlene's name was mentioned.

"Well, I have to get back," Sheehan said. "If you need me, holler."

Sheehan left.

"I'm sorry I have to talk to you about this," Benton said.

"It's not just that," the woman said. "It's that Darlene is gone and whoever murdered her is free. It's not fair."

Benton nodded. "Do you know who was the last to see her?"

Benton remembered it was Valerie Perry from the police report. But it was always better to play deaf and dumb. You never knew what people would tell you.

"Me," she said. "We were working late on a job."

"What was that?"

"Test processing. We had a big job to turn out by the next day and we worked late all week. The last time I saw her was about eight o'clock."

"Did she say anything unusual to you that day—or the days before."

"Like what?"

"Maybe that she felt like she was being watched."

"She was."

Benton blinked.

"I mean, she was a pretty girl and people often watched. At that time there were all kinds of construction workers. They were installing new wire in the ceiling and walls, and she did say that she felt she was being watched. But not that she was worried about it or anything. Just aware of it."

"You mean, uh, she as being ogled?"

"Yes."

"When did you first become aware she was missing?"

Another shadow passed across Valerie Perry's face. "That night about ten. Her husband, Dave, called me, said she wasn't home yet, and asked if she was still here. He knew she was working late."

She paused.

"I got scared right away, because she only lived in Howell, about fifteen minutes away. If she had car trouble she could call. It wouldn't take her two hours to get home."

"Were you, uh, close to her?"

Valerie Perry nodded.

"Was she close to anyone else here? I mean, might she have talked with someone else if she had something on her mind."

"Well, there's, uh, Krista."

"Krista?"

"Krista Gass. Another text processor. But I don't think she'd know anything more than me."

"Could I speak to her?"

"She's out today. She'll be in tomorrow."

"I'll see her then," Benton said, and added, "Do you know where she parked her car?"

"Yes."

"Do you have time to show me?"

Valerie was over to the black girl and said something, then came back to Benton and started to walk in the opposite direction from where he had come, down a carpeted hall equally as long as the one that had led him to her.

"I never did like where she parked," Valerie Perry said. "It's not in the main area, but off to the side of the building."

"Isolated?"

"Yes."

"You figured it might be dangerous?"

"I don't know. Maybe. They have patrols out there, but I don't know . . . with everything you read in the papers."

They went out of the building at a side entrance that was overseen by a white-haired, bespectacled uniform guard. All the guards seemed to wear glasses.

The parking area on the side of the building where Darlene had parked was much less crowded with cars than the front of the building. *But it's not exactly Timbuktu either,* Benton thought.

"She always parked here," Valerie Perry said, standing on one diagonally marked space and pointing to another.

"What kind of car did she have?"

"Chevrolet Impala. Red. Nice car. They found that abandoned."

They stood a moment and regarded the empty space, almost, Benton thought, as if awaiting the return of Darlene Santora. For a moment Benton believed it, and then he thought of the 8 x 10's of her and was jogged back into reality.

"Could you show me her office now?"

They went back into the building. The guard who had been on the desk was just down the hall, his arms crossed, staring out through the one-way windows at the parking lot. It occurred to Benton that security would not be impossible to breach here. Not at all.

"This is it," Valerie Perry said, standing outside an illuminated but empty office across the corridor from the main text processing room.

"Thanks," Benton said. "I don't think I need you right now. But I would like to meet with Krista tomorrow."

"Just drop back later and I'll arrange it."

"Thank you."

The office was empty except for a gray desk and a chair.

He tried the desk drawers—three on each side and a long flat one in the middle.

The entire contents of the six drawers were a paper clip and, from the back of one on the left, a sugar packet from McDonald's, the last remnants of Darlene Santora.

After a while he left.

*   *   *

At dark, Benton was sitting in his car in the side parking lot, watching the occasional person come around the corner of the building, get in a car, and drive away.

Benton had decided against trying to talk with any of them. He sensed that it wouldn't do any good.

Or, to put it another way, he sensed something of the killer: no one would have seen him; he would have made sure of that.

All Benton wanted to do was observe. He didn't really know what he was looking for. All he knew was that the facts of all the cases were inside him, and if there was a connection to be made it would just happen.

He was still sitting there at ten o'clock. No one had come out of the building for a half hour, but he had been checked once by security.

He left the parking lot at a quarter after ten, thinking that he had come up with nothing.

But there was something, and he had missed it. Normally, he would pay attention to the vague, fleeting ideas that sped along a thin line between conscious and unconscious thinking. That was where insights could come from; that's where solutions could come from.

Such an idea had flitted across his mind as he had walked the empty corridors with Valerie Perry. It was a connection, but it had been there and gone in a millisecond.

He drove down Route 9 to find a motel, contemplating what his next move would be.

CHAPTER 27

Downstairs, in a corner of a finished basement that was shielded from the rest of the basement by partition walls, Albert Brooks slowly stripped off his clothes, preparatory to putting on his exercise shorts and top.

Against one wall he had mounted a tall mirror; he liked to look at himself when he exercised. Indeed, he liked to look at himself all the time.

His body, he knew, was a work of art, as muscularly lean as a prizefighter's. He was sixteen now, would be seventeen in a month, and he had started exercising when he was twelve. At first he had worked out with weights but quickly had perceived that once you stopped lifting the muscle would turn to fat. He had seen more than one slob around who had formerly been a weight lifter.

So he decided to build himself up naturally, inch by inch, solid muscle that would never go away.

Every morning since, he had done exercises: running,

187

sit-ups, one- and two-handed push-ups, pull-ups. At this point in his development he felt like he could drive spikes with his bare fists.

Stripped, he looked at himself in the mirror.

He was about six foot and weighed one seventy. He was perfectly developed, and relatively hairless, just a few blond hairs on his chest.

He had two tattoos. One on his upper left arm that was a US Marine insignia and said "USMC Forever." He had gotten that when he was fourteen after seeing a John Wayne picture.

The other was of a leopard crawling on the top of his right arm, its claws and teeth bloody. Albert admired the leopard: he was strong and fast and merciless, a very dangerous creature.

The face didn't fit the body. One might expect a hard, handsome face above such a body, but it wasn't. Instead Albert resembled Howdy Doody or the What-Me-Worry character—Alfred E. Neumann—in *Mad* magazine. His eyes were large, blue, and far apart, he had freckles around a flattish nose, and a wide mouth, and he had large teeth, with a space between the front two. His ears stuck out.

Girls considered him cute, and he had no trouble getting dates with them.

Tonight he was going out with Tracy Martin, who, like him, had been thrown out of Poughkeepsie High. Tracy was a hot number, always good for when he couldn't find anyone else and needed a place to drop a load.

He dropped to the floor and rhythmically started to do one-arm push-ups.

He did thirty with the right arm and thirty with the left, the last two with a little difficulty.

Fifteen minutes later his exercise regimen was completed. He was covered with a sheen of sweat and felt, as usual, terrific.

Still nude, he walked across the basement toward a shower in the corner. He felt like a leopard.

Halfway across the basement he stopped when he heard a noise. A squeak.

That would be Mrs. Baker, and the old cunt who, with her loving husband, Harold, had been his foster parents for the last two years. They, like the other three families, had wanted him to live with them because they got an allowance from the state.

He went into the shower and turned on the water.

Two months earlier they had sat him down and told him that when he was seventeen he would have to leave. They couldn't handle him; they were too old. But they would always be there to help him if he needed it.

Albert's attitude was simple: Fuck 'em. Once he walked out of the door he would never come back, except maybe to rob them.

He had done that with the Keenans, the last foster family before the Bakers. It had been perfect. He knew the layout of the house, where the valuables were, their habits, everything. He had been able to come in there one night when they were away on vacation and take jewelry, valuables, and some cash for a grand haul of three grand. And no one had been the wiser. Indeed, if the cops had come, or one of the Keenans had unexpectedly returned, he could have claimed he had just come to the house because he missed them. Cry a little. Poor little boy. No sweat.

He had briefly considered robbing the Tartaglias and the Kennedy, the other two foster families, but had decided against it. It had been too long since he had been there.

Things could have changed to the point where he would be at risk without knowing it. So he didn't.

Plus, they had a motherfucker for a district attorney. When they had caught him for setting fire to a chicken coop and all the chickens had been killed the DA tried like hell to get him tried as an adult offender. Albert figured he was much cleverer today than he had been in those days and likely wouldn't get caught, but there was always the possibility.

After the shower, he went back to the exercise corner. There was a closed and locked closet he used. He got the key from his pants pocket and opened it up.

The shelves were filled with his special stuff. Stuff he had sent away for. Some knives and handcuffs and detective badges—and undergarments that he had stolen off lines and, lately, from inside homes. He loved to crush them against his face. Sometimes he was able to detect the faint woman smells and feel power over them.

The upper shelves were filled with the detective magazines that he had started collecting when he was fourteen.

He had never thrown a single one out, and he loved perusing them, poring over the stories, reading the details of the crimes, and the pursuits.

Some stories turned him on. The ones where the women were in bondage, completely at the mercy of their killers before they were killed.

He tried to imagine what the women went through before they died. What they said, how they cried and begged, how the killer was in complete mastery over them, what stupid sluts they were and how they deserved to die. That was one thing most of the stories never said: that the women deserved to die.

He imagined how he would have done it had he been the killer.

A lot of the killers had been caught. He wouldn't have been. Most cops were stupid and couldn't find their ass in the dark. They would be easy to fool.

He took the top issue from one of the piles. It was a *Master Detective*, two years old.

On the cover was a blond cunt lying on a bed with her hands tied behind her back, her face a mask of fear. Looming in the dark background was the silhouette of a figure, light shining off the silvery blade of a knife.

He had this cunt just where he wanted her.

Albert put the magazine back, closed and locked the closet door, and sat down in a straight-back chair.

He spread his legs, closed his eyes, and pictured himself with the blonde in the room.

She would be screaming, farting, crying, begging.

He slipped his hand around his penis, which was rock hard. He had her just where he wanted her. She was a cunt; he was her master.

That night, at dusk, Albert Brooks and Tracy Martin drove in Albert's souped-up 1963 Impala with the chrome and striped wheels toward Mahler's Drive-In Theater.

Brooks was thinking that even though Tracy was just a cunt, he liked her. She appreciated Albert, knew that he was going places, that someday he would be a force to be reckoned with. That his working on the garbage truck for the last six months was only temporary. That he would go to college and make a tremendous amount of money and have the respect and admiration of everyone. It was only a matter of time.

"So what did you do today, Albert?" she asked.

"I started looking into colleges to go to."

"Really? Where are you looking?"

"Harvard, Yale, Princeton, schools like that."

"Oh," Tracy said. "They're hard to get into, aren't they?"

"Not if you have the brains and money," Albert said. "I'll get in."

Tracy said nothing.

"Right?" Albert said, and glanced at Tracy.

She looked at him and nodded. "Sure," she said.

Albert wasn't sure if he had detected a trace of sarcasm. He felt something molten and hot come up inside him, but after a while it went away, to a degree.

He was always angry, or at least that's what the last school psychiatrist had told him: "You always seem to be angry, Albert. What's the problem?"

"I'm not always angry," he had told the psychiatrist. What assholes psychiatrists and guidance counselors were!

Albert parked in the back of the lot, which wasn't crowded.

There were two Westerns playing at the drive-in. They promised to be very boring. It didn't matter. Albert didn't go there to watch movies.

The first movie, called *Ulzana's Raid*, started at dusk. It was with Burt Lancaster.

Albert liked Lancaster. For one thing, they had the same nickname—Burt—though spelled differently. For another, Lancaster was a very tough guy, like Albert. He could take anything.

For some reason, this movie held Albert's interest better than most Westerns. There was something different about it that he couldn't quite put his finger on.

Something about the Indians. They were more dangerous, more vicious than in usual Hollywood Westerns. In most, the Indians acted mean, but you could tell they were acting.

In this movie you couldn't tell. They were vicious, and seemed that way. Albert found himself involved, excited. He was anticipating what they would do.

About halfway through the movie they came through. It was a scene that made Tracy Martin turn her head from the screen.

A bunch of them killed a farmer, then they were huddled around him so you didn't know what they were doing. Then they sprang back triumphantly and a moment later were playing catch with his freshly removed heart.

"Ugh," Tracy said.

Albert's penis was as hard as a rock.

CHAPTER 28

Benton was in his room in a motel in downtown Holmdel. He had Lawless on the phone.

"The people on the task force were starting to flake away now," Lawless said. "I figure we can hold them another few days."

"Who can we hold after that?"

"Barbara will still be on it, and so will Piccolo and Edmunton. And I'll stay with it as much as I can."

There was a pause.

"Thanksgiving's coming up," Lawless said. "What are you going to be doing?"

"Work through," Benton said. "I wouldn't enjoy the turkey much knowing this maniac's still out there."

"Well, Barbara and I are having a little get-together at her place. If you can make it, please do."

"Thanks, Joe," Benton said. "Thanks a lot. I will if I can."

But both knew he wouldn't.

Benton and Lawless said good-bye and then hung up.

Benton got his briefcase from the closet and brought it over to the bed. Over the past two weeks he had probed the other most recent killings, starting with Clifton, then Parsippany, Old Bridge, then at the College of Staten Island. Tomorrow he was going to be visiting Holmdel, the other AT&T facility that had a victim.

He had collected a lot of paper. He had interviewed, as diplomatically as possible, officers investigating the cases. While trying to determine just how deep and thorough their investigations were, he had learned additional facts on the cases that had not yet been sent to the FBI.

Some of the investigative work he thought was shoddy, but in the final analysis he wondered just how successful they would have been anyway. They were up against a very clever killer who did his homework.

Benton got a hollow feeling in his stomach. He wondered how successful he would be.

So far, he had been virtually engulfed with data, and he had the feeling that he was no closer to the killer than the first time he saw Michelle Reynolds.

But he told himself that that's the way homicide was. Miles and miles of boring, endless trivia and garbage interrupted by moments of sheer joy. A case established a history of failure and frustration, and you could feel you would never solve one again. It all looked insurmountable.

And then there would be a new piece of evidence, an insight, maybe a tip—and you would clear the case in a matter of hours.

The thing was not to get discouraged.

Benton tried to think positive now, but he simply didn't feel it.

He had been at it fourteen hours a day and more since the case started.

He went through all the material he had on the cases twice more, then returned everything to his briefcase.

Sometimes, he thought, he could get a fresh eye on a case by staying away from it for a few days and then reapproaching it. He had done that successfully a number of times.

But in this case that was clearly not the way to go. It was a luxury he could not afford.

He put the briefcase back in the closet and closed the door. Across the room, above the double bed, was a painting of a country scene: a field of wheat or corn or something. In the foreground was a board fence and above was a blue sky and a golden sun.

It was supposed to be cheerful and bright; Benton thought of it as dark and somber, the perfect place to bury a body.

Christ.

He smiled. The Bent One. How many people in the world would look at a bucolic painting and think of it as a place to bury someone?

Other people—most people—would think positive thoughts about it.

He remembered what Dr. Stern had said: "You know, we live in a projected world. It's like a half glass of water. Some people would think of the glass as half empty, and the others as half full."

There were times in his life when he certainly had to regard life as being half empty—like the times when he was having electricity shot through his fucking brain!

And all those bad days with Joyce, and the despair he felt that day when he saw what had also happened to Beth, how she now looked at him.

Still, he looked at life with endless hope, that it would all have a happy ending.

Thought: what Steinbeck said. If men knew how their lives would turn out they would kill themselves.

He was saying that no matter how you live, in the end you die, so life is, de facto, unhappy. There are no happy endings.

Benton had thought about killing himself. He remembered once, just before he took on the Franconi case, he was standing by a window watching the leaves about to blow away. And that's when he felt his life had been reduced to. A dried-up leaf waiting for the final gust of wind to blow him away.

And then Lawless had called, just like before this case, and he was okay again.

He would not kill himself, though, of that he was sure. He just didn't know why, but he knew he wouldn't.

Maybe. Ho-ho.

He wondered if the killer ever thought about killing himself. Benton did not know, but he wouldn't bet against it. Murder and suicide were close, real close. One was violence against others. One was against yourself.

Insight: a projected world. How easy it would be to take all the bad feelings about yourself and project them into the world. Then kill the world to eliminate the feelings.

He got up and stripped and noticed for the first time that his clothing was fitting more loosely on him than ever before. He had probably dropped ten pounds since the case started.

He had either lost the weight from not eating much or he was terminally fucking ill.

He went into the shower and was halfway through rinsing himself off when the insight occurred, and he was so gripped by it that he only half dried himself off. He went into the bedroom and immediately to the closet and took his briefcase out.

He put it on the bed, where he spread out the papers and leafed through them.

The insight had been about Ted Bundy's Volkswagen.

The cops in Florida had gotten hold of it, and the thing that struck them was that the rear seat was missing. They asked Bundy why it was that way and he could never really explain it.

But the cops knew why it was taken out: It was to make room for bodies.

Benton checked the victims' cars that had been recovered, though he didn't need to. He knew what kinds of cars they had; this was just a neurotic glich, like a miser recounting money he has counted a thousand times.

Benton had seen four of the cars and they, and all the rest, all had one thing in common: No seats needed to be removed. There was plenty of room in back to transport a body—or, more to the point, to hide a killer.

It hung together.

All the attacks were at night. Darkness. The killer could have gotten into the cars when it was dark. Then he would lie waiting in the back until the victim got into the car and started it up.

Benton blinked. He thought of the young girl he had seen in the 7-Eleven store. What might her reaction be?

Okay, assume that's true.

He gets into the car, waits in the back.

Wait. How does he get in the car?

Some people would leave the door open. Others?

A slim jim could open most cars. And this guy could get the hardware to open others.

It would be easy to control the girls if he had a weapon. Just tell them to drive to a certain place. Or maybe take over himself.

Except: What if the victim came out with a friend? He hadn't killed two people who knew each other. He would have to be lucky or have done his homework and know that the victim would enter her car alone.

That he only killed single victims was an assumption. Serial murderers weren't against killing multiples. Kemper killed two young girls the first time he struck. Lucas killed a few at a time; entire families had been slaughtered.

It was just that the bodies, if done, hadn't been found.

Picking victims would take work. Surveillance. At least watching the potential victim a few nights.

A lot of research. She had to be young, blond, and own a car he could get into and hide in. The formula had to be there.

Hanson in Anchorage. He had a formula too. More exacting than this one. But a lot of girls passed his test.

What about security? The AT&T places had it. Then again, the security people weren't usually any good unless they were ex-cops.

The killer could have sat there unnoticed. Or maybe he was in a protected vehicle, like a van. He could stay in the back and not be seen.

Somehow it made sense, though Benton was not familiar with any particular serial killer who used that method.

It took him hours to get to sleep, his mind going over and over the case. He was starting to think of all the victims in another way: all of them had been robbed of their right to live by the killer. Hundreds and hundreds of years just snuffed out. No, thousands. Kids that would never be, and their kids. A small army of humanity would not live because of this killer.

Benton inhaled sharply. Christ, he wished he could get him.

CHAPTER 29

It was snowing when Benton awoke the next morning, a persistent falling that coated the parking lot and beyond in a thin coat of white.

The sky was mostly gray, but there was a little blue in the distance.

Benton had always liked rough weather, at least when he was inside, but today he didn't. He felt a certain tightness. From long experience he had learned one anti-dote was work, so he got to it at nine o'clock, the earliest he figured he should call to try to determine if one of the security people at the abduction sites had spotted someone lingering in the parking lot and had reported it. It was a long shot, but you never knew.

He called Freehold AT&T first.

They said they would get back to him.

He called security at the College of Staten Island. They also told him they would get back to him.

There was no simple way to check security at the Electric Pussy Cat in Old Bridge or some of the other places. If necessary, he would have to go there and try to dredge up witnesses.

He waited until ten-thirty when the Freehold security chief, Sheehan, got back to him.

He told Benton that nothing unusual had been logged at any time on the last night that Darlene Santora had been seen alive.

Benton waited until eleven for security at the College of Staten Island to call back, but no one did. He left a message at the desk that someone might call, and left for Holmdel.

The snow had stopped by the time he reached the Holmdel facility of AT&T. The idea that someone might have been spotted watching the facility here lessened considerably. The place was huge, at least a quarter of a mile long and one hundred yards wide and six or seven stories high—a big glass box. It looked like the parking lot was big enough to handle the cars from Shea Stadium.

Benton drove around it twice, noting a series of sweeping, interconnecting paths. It looked like there were four main entrances. He went in the one with the flags out front.

Inside was even more impressive. The roof was tinted glass, and the core was open space with various facilities laid out on the floor. The offices themselves, it seemed, ran around the perimeter of the building, with walkways across the vast emptiness in the interior.

Fortunately he had called ahead, so it only took him a few minutes to get access to the place. He followed the security chief, a small, dark-haired woman named King, into a glass elevator that they rode to the third floor, then walked a hundred yards or so to aisle G and to office G 115, where Rosalinde Berne had worked.

The office was occupied by a young dark-haired man whose name, Benton had noticed on the nameplate outside, was Eric Johnson.

The security chief explained who Benton was, and then left. Johnson took Benton to meet people who had known Ms. Berne.

Benton talked with the people—two who were programmers, as Berne had been, and her supervisor—for an hour.

A significant detail emerged: one of the women had walked through the parking lot at around seven-thirty and had seen Rosalinde get into her car, an '83 Nova.

It was still daylight at that time so it was unlikely that the killer had been hiding in the back of the car.

Rosalinde Berne had lived alone, and after she left work no one seemed to know what had happened to her. The next thing anyone knew, she was dead.

The snow had stopped, and the sun had come out when Benton left Holmdel at around three o'clock.

His next stop would be Monmouth College, but he decided to put that off until he could first reach someone by phone.

He drove back to the motel and lay down on the bed. Before he realized it, he was asleep.

Benton awoke at around eleven o'clock. He lay on the bed and thought about his mother and father.

How many times, he thought, he had wanted them to be with him at various important moments in his life.

All his birthdays, and the day he graduated from the academy, and the day he got his gold shield, and all the other times he wanted them to be with him . . . they simply weren't there.

He smiled. They were at his wedding, he would give them that.

He wondered again about this most bizarre creature, the lustmurderer.

What in God's name could have produced him? What could make him want to take a sharp instrument and cut flesh open and mutilate genitals? Christ, when you thought about it, what the hell was he accomplishing by cutting body parts off?

Power. It had to be a power trip of some sort. Control, right? He had seen that over and over again in rape cases. The rapists liked to dominate and control; sex was just a means to do that.

Lustmurderers didn't rape, they cut.

Indians—Indians would do that. Cut off the scalp of the victim, show that they completely dominated the victim.

That was what they were doing, wasn't it?

Same thing here.

But why the need to dominate and control. What did that do for them? What exactly did the killing do for them?

Benton thought of Carl Panzram, a serial murderer in the 1930s who had killed twenty-one people, including young boys and men. He liked to strangle them or beat them to death.

Benton smiled.

Carl was one angry dude, he thought. Just before they put him in the chair he said something like he wished he had more time so he could kill more.

That was pissed.

Maybe anger was the answer, maybe it wasn't domination and control.

Bundy had been angry. He had hit one of the girls in the

sorority so hard they found brain matter splashed up on the ceiling.

The Yorkshire Ripper was angry . . . Brudos was angry . . . Armstrong was angry . . . they were all angry. You had to be angry to take someone's life against their will.

And not care. Not a single serial murderer he knew of had ever expressed remorse. Indeed, Bundy couldn't understand why they were making such a fuss over missing girls.

But what was at the core?

What's at my core? Benton thought. And he immediately thought; *Nada*, and smiled, because these days he wasn't believing that. There was something there. A good detective, anyway.

Still, he hadn't solved this case, so how good was he?

He felt a little something crawling inside.

Benton left his room about midnight. Snow had started falling lightly again, but he figured it wouldn't hamper what he wanted to do.

He wanted to drive, possibly taking the same route the killer took at night, a likely time when he drove it.

His car was parked under a light in the parking lot, and before he got in he checked the back seat. Even with the light shining into the car it would have been easy, because of the way the shadows were cast, for someone to secure himself there.

He drove north on the Garden State Parkway to the Alfred C. Driscoll Bridge, which spanned the Raritan River. He had seen this river in daylight, and its shores were lined with industrial plants which, Benton knew, dumped their waste in the river.

Now the river was dark, the only lights from the plants

on the shores. Above a number of the plants large plumes
of smoke coiled skyward.

You wouldn't want to whiff that shit, Benton thought,
*without wearing a grade-three mask, unless you wanted to
check out.*

Benton tensed a bit as got off the bridge onto Route 440
north. Nearby, the body of Anne-Jacobs, the student in
Staten Island, had been found.

Traffic was relatively light. He drove in the middle of
the three lanes. It was a dark road.

The body had been found under a bridge, fifteen feet
into the brush on the Southbound side.

It would have been easy for the killer to stop the car
under a bridge—no one could see him from above—and
then simply drag the girl out into the greenery. A big ten
seconds. No sweat.

The body had been found under the first bridge as you
approach the Fresh Kills dump.

Benton knew when he started to get close. There was a
garbagy perfume smell—maybe like rotting fruit—that
seeped into the car.

He looked to the left as he drove. He slowed down the
car and a truck barreled by.

The dump loomed large, an immense, fenced-off hill of
man-made garbage, on top of which, silhouetted against
the sky, were a couple of bulldozers.

Benton glanced in the rearview mirror. There was no
one behind him. He slowed down and looked at the bridge
under which the body had been found. *Yes,* he thought *it
wouldn't have been too risky to drop her body there.*

The smell faded as he went farther north.

*Far up to his left there was some sort of big industrial
plant with a massive stack pouring smoke into the sky.*

206

A few minutes later he took a fork off 440 onto the Staten Island Expressway. It was a little more crowded than 440, but it wasn't exactly bustling with life.

He glanced to the left and right. Mostly private homes, but also some apartment houses, were nestled in the low hills, now white with snow. Benton had never been to Sicily, but he would bet that the largely Italian population of the borough had settled in Staten Island because it reminded them of home.

He thought: *Isn't it weird? We all keep going home, no matter what home was like.*

So many times perps on the run had been caught because the cops simply went to where they lived and waited for them to come home.

A lot.

You can't go home again, but we always try.

An image: Maybe four years ago, after his mother and father had moved to California and he was feeling very low, he had gone down to the apartment building on East 74th where he had been raised, stood across the street, and looked at it. He wanted something from it, and after a while he figured it out: he wanted those carefree, worry-free days to return, even though that's not how his childhood had been. There had been a lot of anxiety. But he didn't remember that. He just remembered that he had been taken care of.

He never got whatever it was he was looking for. He wondered if the killer did.

He wondered if this killer ever went home looking for something.

To his right he saw the tops of buildings of the College of Staten Island, all square and ordinary-looking except one that looked like a multi-winged butterfly had landed.

He had found, when he went there, that it was the library—where the victim had worked.

The killer, Benton thought, had to be using the expressway frequently. Had to. It was a route that led to towns where there had been victims: the expressway led to 440 south, and from there he could get off on Route 9 and hit Old Bridge, Freehold—and if he continued down the Garden State he would hit Holmdel.

And, of course, there was the College of Staten Island; that was directly on the route.

The top of the Verrazano-Narrows Bridge suddenly loomed up over the low hills. Benton knew he was going to have a decision to make. From the Verrazano he could get to any of the other boroughs.

The computer sign welcomed him: 2:02 A.M.—HAVE A NICE DAY—and he smiled back.

You too.

He leapt in the middle lane as he crossed the bridge, which had one of the better views of the tip of Manhattan. He could see the Statue of Liberty, small and green, in the harbor, and the great twin towers of the World Trade Center. Once, he and Joyce had eaten with a friend at Windows on the World.

There was no connection, thus far, of the killer with Manhattan. Only the Bronx. He would go there.

He had a variety of ways to go. Across 278 in Manhattan and then up to the Bronx, or across the Belt Parkway, then the Cross Island Parkway and over the Throgs Neck Bridge to the Bronx.

"Serial killers," Jim Brosnan had said, "love to drive—just drive and drive and drive."

And if you had a body in the back, Benton thought, *wouldn't you want to take the least busy way?*

208

He flicked on his left signal, which was hardly necessary because there was no one behind him, and took the left lane onto the Belt Parkway ramp.

A couple of freighters were berthed under the bridge, and one oil tanker. In all the times he had traveled the Belt he had never seen a good-looking ship in the Narrows. All were ugly and functional.

He wondered what the killer thought when he saw ships in the Narrows.

There was no question that if you liked driving, the Belt was the way to go. It girdled Brooklyn—but they couldn't very well call it the Girdle Parkway—and it was a long drive.

Benton remembered a case, back in the time tunnel, when Seedman was chief of detectives.

A girl had been driving along the Belt and had gotten shot and killed. Unbelievably enough, they cleared the case: somebody had been shooting a .22 far across the water in Manhattan, and the girl had been killed by a stray bullet.

You never knew what you could solve.

Benton crossed over the Throgs Neck Bridge into the Bronx. He took the Cross Bronx Expressway to Webster Avenue, then drove north on Webster until he reached Snake Hill.

He drove up it to the mouth of St. Bonaventure and stopped.

The street was deserted, and he was sure that if he had a body in the back of the car he could drive down it, dump the body, arrange it, and get away with no problem whatsoever.

He drove down the block and parked at the curb a few yards from where the body had been found.

He looked around, glanced in the rearview mirror, and got out. He walked over to where it had been and looked down.

It was as if the girl had never existed.

He turned and looked back down the block toward Snake Hill.

Surveillance had been lifted. He wondered if the perp had been back.

He walked slowly back down the block, aware of where his wadcutter was. He was less concerned with running into the lustmurderer than he was of meeting one of the other predators in the precinct.

He came to the end of the block and looked down Snake Hill. It seemed, again, just like a canyon in some dark mountain pass, only the occasional lights in the apartment buildings violating the illusion.

He started walking back to the car, and as he did he started to feel a little depressed. He knew—just knew—that this guy would kill again, and though he had learned a lot about the killer and how he operated, he was still nowhere near making a collar. The guy was still loose.

He got into his car, and five minutes later was on the Cross Bronx Expressway, heading back toward Jersey. This time he would take the Turnpike south.

Soon he was on it, tooling through the great underbelly of New Jersey, the road lined with factories belching crap and smells and God knew what else, the area that had earned Jersey the distinction of being the only state that glowed in the dark.

He asked himself if there was something he had missed. He had a vague feeling that there was, but he didn't know what. He tried to let his mind go blank for a long time, but

210

it didn't work. If there was something, he didn't know what it was.

Was there something he could learn about this killer, this Henry the Eighth, from other serial murderers?

Yes, don't be around when they're pissed.

He smiled, flicked on the radio, and worked the dial until some soft classical music came on.

Other killers occurred to him, and what they did, and didn't, do.

How did they trap victims? Like this guy?

Gacy played cop, luring kids back to his house.

Corrl picked kids up.

Peter Sutcliffe, the Yorkshire Ripper, trailed women and attacked them.

The Ripper did that too.

Bundy? Slick, he liked to work out plans, pick up girls or invade their houses. Kill them in bed.

Hanson went for prostitutes. So did Bianchi: he and his cousin used to pick them up in their cars.

On the other hand, Bianchi also lured two girls to an empty house and killed them there when he was working in Bellingham, Washington. Benton remembered they found one of the women's pubic hair on the stairs.

Interesting, Benton thought. *Bundy and Bianchi and Gacy made out like they were cops.*

So what did that mean?

Nothing Benton could see.

Jack the Ripper? He accosted the victims in the street.

Carl Panram. Vagabond. Just take a victim at the moment of opportunity.

Armstrong? Hitchhikers. He would pick his victims up.

Kemper did that. He'd pick up girls, and when coeds

were warned not to get into strangers' cars he put a sticker on his car saying he worked at the college.

Heirens. He would invade someone's house.

Harvey Glapton, the photographer, would advertise for girls as models, and once he had them he would bind, photograph, and kill them, then dump their bodies in the desert.

Henry Lee Lucas would kill as the opportunity presented itself.

Benton had a fantasy: a dinner, and at it would be every serial murderer and mass murderer that ever was. They'd need a big hall.

Ho-ho. Who would be the guest of honor?

Fish, Albert Fish. Did they come any slicker than Albert Fish? Kemper was right up there, and Jack the Ripper wasn't exactly a vessel of wellness.

What would they serve?

The Bent One, he thought. *The Bent One*.

One minute later he was looking at a purplish cloud that seemed to envelope one of the factories when a thought occurred to him that made him blink—and his mind race.

Not all victims, he thought *were victims. Some got away.* No serial murderer would succeed every time he went on the hunt. Some girls lived. They lived because they were tough, or lucky, or in some way could defend themselves.

Plenty of girls got away.

Jesus, maybe some escaped this guy.

Maybe someone had a complaint.

Freehold. The Bronx.

They could go through the complaints fairly quickly in Freehold. The Bronx might be another story.

Benton hated to wake Lawless at this time of the morning.

But he would.

CHAPTER 30

Jane Nolan was a pretty, blond-haired woman in her late twenties, but a frown twisted her face as she made her way across the darkened parking lot toward her car.

She was annoyed. No matter how many times she had told Luisa, who worked with her in the office, how to file, she just wasn't learning it. There was no question in Jane's mind that Hispanics and blacks had some sort of cultural lack that damaged their ability to do exacting work. Their minds always seemed to be somewhere else.

Of course, Jane knew that she wasn't the easiest person to work for. She was demanding, in fact, but working as assistant to the financial aid director of the Bronx Community College was an exacting kind of job. When the government reviewed the application forms, they wanted and demanded precision. And that's what Jane was good at—making sure that all the *t*'s were crossed and the *i*'s dotted. If things were not right, you could depend on Jane Nolan to spot it.

213

Then again, Jane thought, she didn't demand the kind of efficiency that she herself was capable of. Just ordinary competency would be all right, but Luisa Peres hadn't achieved that, and Jane didn't know exactly how to handle it.

Her mind flicked to the latest incident, today. Luisa had misplaced three FAF applications, and it had taken Jane a half hour to find them. It was one thing to misfile them, but it was quite another to have no memory, no clue, to where you might have put them.

Darn, Jane thought. *She should be at least a little observant and attentive.*

It was this quality of mind that made Jane notice something that was different about her car, a 1983 Toyota, from the way it had been in the morning.

Though the car was in shadow, out of the orbit of the occasional street lamps that illuminated the lot, she could see part of a seat belt jutting out the bottom of the rear door. Just a bit of it.

She had not done that, and her stomach sank as she realized that somebody had been in the car.

Instantly her mind scanned, but she realized that she had left nothing of value in the car. You don't leave things in your car in the Bronx, even in a parking lot where there's a security guard.

She came up to the car, peered into the front, and was about to open the rear door with her key but didn't. Something stopped her, and then suddenly her body was covered with gooseflesh and she silently gasped and glanced around. There was no one. All she could see was the top of the kiosk where the security guard was.

She swallowed a scream and forced herself to look nonchalant as she started to walk away from the car.

There was someone in there. She had been able to see the paleness of a face in the darkness of the car.

She came into full view of the kiosk and then looked back. There was no sign of anyone.

She came up to the kiosk. The black uniformed security guard was there, standing outside.

"There's someone in my car," she said.

He frowned. "Where?"

"In the back. On the floor."

He hesitated a moment, then reached into the kiosk and came up with a long club. With this in one hand and a large flashlight in the other, he said, "Let's go."

She led him down an aisle of cars and then to her own car. As she approached it she immediately noticed something.

The rear door had been opened.

The guard went up to the car and shone the light through the side rear window, then to the front. His club was at the ready. "There's no one here," he said.

"There was!"

He nodded. "Well, don't worry about it. There's no one there now. You can drive home."

She hesitated.

"Shouldn't we call the police?"

"I'll take care of that," he said. "You just get in your car and drive home."

She hesitated, but then opened the door and got in.

"Lock the doors," he said.

She did.

He waved.

The guard, whose name was William Richards, walked back to the kiosk and went inside.

He looked at the phone.

No way, he thought. No way was he going to call the police. He didn't want to have to start explaining how somebody got in over the fence without his seeing. Jobs were too valuable.

If the lady asked him about it he'd tell her the police had caught someone prowling around another parking area.

No big deal.

CHAPTER 31

Albert Brooks III, nude, in the basement of his home in the Bronx, completed his 150th push-up and sprang to his feet. There was no sign of sweat on his body, which was something to marvel at: he was muscular, almost etched, but not grossly so. His body was the result of natural exercise and healthy living.

He sat down on a straight back chair and tried to relax, but couldn't.

And then Ray, who lived inside his head, spoke.

Asshole. You let the cunt get away. She's laughing at you now, stupid. You put three days into tracking this bitch, and what happens. Nothing. You are pathetic.

"I did the best I could," Albert said softly but out loud. "She was lucky."

Luck has nothing to do with it. You didn't plan well enough. You're an asshole.

Albert felt a depression settling over him. Ray could make him so depressed, and Ray could be so cruel. But Albert thought he had done well, very well in the past.

He turned his head and looked across the basement. It was dark except for the single light above his exercise area at the freezer, which was in a corner of the room. He got up and padded over to it.

He manipulated the combination lock, took it off, and lifted the lid. The freezer was about two-thirds full of fish and other health food, and the other third contained carefully wrapped heads and organs.

He picked up a head and looked at it. It was hard to see through the plastic wrap because of the frost, but then Albert wiped it off.

It was remarkably preserved. If you looked close you could even tell the color of the eyes.

"I did well," Albert said.

You did well in the past, Ray said, *but this is the present. Don't tell me what you did yesterday, show me today. Get it?*

Albert felt white-hot rage soaring up inside him, but he said nothing. He closed the lid, relocked it, and went back to the exercise area.

He sat back down in the straight-back chair, closed his eyes, and started to think.

I am slick, he told himself, *as slick as anyone who ever lived.*

Yes, he was. He was no asshole.

How many times, when he had suddenly appeared in the back of a car, or the times he had walked up to one of them, had the girl been scared, very scared? And how he had conned them into thinking that nothing was going to happen to them. He remembered one, the dancing cunt in Old Bridge.

When he got her in the car, he told her that he meant her

no harm, that he just wanted a little sex, that he would be very gentle and even pay her.

She had believed him for a while.

He glanced down. He was getting erect.

He had held the gun on her, but had dipped it down a bit so that she would think he was a little relaxed about it, but not so relaxed that she would try to escape.

And then, when they were in the field, he had told her to strip, and she had, and he had put the gun down and had approached her, and she had tears in her eyes and started to fart, and then he had told her to turn around and had looped the 4-pair over her neck and a minute later she dropped to the ground dead.

He was three-quarters erect.

Then he had gone to his van and had brought her back, like all the others, and had taken out his ax and knife and had started to work on her. He had worked on her in the basement where he was afraid when he was young.

Albert pictured it in vivid detail. Her helpless body, his powerful body, and the knife cutting into her, chopping her head off. He was in total control, and then he stuck his hands into the wounds he had made, exploring and solving her secret places and smelling her innards and rubbing her on him. . . . He stroked furiously and came fifteen seconds later.

He reached down, picked up a pair of bikini panties he had placed on the floor, and wiped himself off.

He felt better, but then Ray spoke.

You're still an asshole, Albert. Yesterday is yesterday, today is today.

Albert said nothing.

CHAPTER 32

In response to Benton's late-night call, Lawless had detectives checking out assault complaints in the Five Three and adjacent precincts, the theory being that the killer, if he assaulted someone in the Bronx, might have done it in the Five Three or other precincts close to the area where the body was dumped simply because he knew those areas well. At least this was the theory.

Citywide, of course, there had been many complaints, and it wouldn't be possible to check all of them.

Benton's task was simpler. In Freehold there had been three assault complaints. Two were girls assaulted outside bars, and the other was an employee of a shoe store in a shopping center. One had occurred a week, two weeks, and another only three days before Darlene Santora had been killed.

Benton checked out the assault closest to the killing date first.

It was a young blond woman named Rita Kenney. She had been assaulted outside a bar where she worked as a barmaid. She told Benton that the guy who assaulted her was about fifty-five and "drunk as a skunk" when he started pawing her outside. The assault consisted of that and a slap in the face.

It definitely did not sound like the perp.

The second case was the one that had occurred two weeks before the killing.

Here, the suspect sounded sort of right. The woman who had been assaulted—she had been picked up by the guy and assaulted in his car—said he was a young, well-built, light-haired guy, maybe twenty-five. When she wouldn't put out he slapped her in the face and she ran away from the car.

The problem was with the victim: she had black hair and was about thirty. All of Henry the Eighth's victims had been younger and blond.

Benton had one complainant left, and it sounded most promising of all. The cop who took the complaint said the incident had started in the parking lot outside the woman's place of employment. She worked in a store called Andrea's, which was in the Freehold Shopping Mall on Route 9. Benton went over there on the night of the 22nd.

As he stood inside the doorway to the store, Benton hoped she wasn't there. There were three people who looked like workers in the store, all female and all dark-haired, not a blond among them. There was a young guy at a cash register behind a counter in front.

If Joanna Vitale—that was the complainant's name—was one of the women present, Benton would be back to square one.

Benton went over to the cashier. "Excuse me," he said, "is Joanna Vitale here?"

The man looked at Benton. "Yes," he said, "she's right over there."

Benton felt something in his stomach move—downward.

He went over to the woman, who he guessed to be about twenty-one. She had jet black hair.

"Excuse me," he said, "my name is George Benton." He showed his badge.

"I wonder if you could help me," he said. "I'm a detective from New York investigating a case down here, and I understand you were assaulted not too long ago."

The woman had intense blue eyes.

"Can I see your ID again?"

Benton had put it back in his jacket pocket.

"Sure."

She took it out and looked it over carefully.

Benton took it back.

"That's what that hump said he was," she said. "A cop."

"Did he show you ID?"

She shook her head.

"Can you tell me exactly what happened?"

"Yeah. Why don't we talk outside."

They came up to the cashier.

"I'll be back in a few minutes," she said to the man at the cash register.

They went outside and stood near the entrance. Benton waited for her to speak.

"I usually get off work at around nine-thirty," she said, "but this night about two weeks ago I wasn't feeling well so I left early. When I got to my car I saw this hump trying to get in."

Benton looked at her.

"I asked what the hell he thought he was doing. He

222

said, 'I'm a police officer. We had a report of you transporting a controlled substance!'

"I didn't believe him and asked for his credentials. He made like he was going into his jacket pocket, and moved toward me. The next thing I knew he grabbed me by the arms—God, he was strong—and told me to get in my car and be quiet or he'd kill me. He said he had a gun.

"For the moment I panicked and obeyed him. We got in the car and he pulled a gun on me. He told me to drive, and I did."

She paused, inhaled sharply.

"He took me out by the old dump site," she said. "I figured he was going to rape me. I didn't know what to do, but I figured the best thing was not to try anything. I figured if I was going to do anything I was only going to get one chance. He was so strong.

"When we got to the dump site I saw a van there. I had hope—I thought someone else was there, but then I realized it was his.

"It really scared me. It was all so planned. He took me by the arm and led me to, like, a woodsy area, and I sensed, as we walked, that he wanted to get behind me.

"I figured I better do something, so at that point I stopped and turned and started to protest to him and whine and all and when I thought his guard was down just a little fit I brought my knee up with all my might and gave him a knife strike on the side of the face—"

"Knife strike?"

"I've been taking karate for a year. Anyway, he went down and I started to run. I figured he'd kill me if he caught me. But you know, I sort of knew the area. When I was a kid we all used to go there, and I found my way through some woods and back roads and got to 505. I made it to a house and called my father."

Benton looked at her.

"What did this guy look like?"

"I'll never forget him. He was at least six feet, but very wiry, and he had light blond hair, a flattish nose, and wide big eyes. And his ears stuck out. His face was pleasant, except when you looked at the eyes."

"What about them?"

"They were mean, crazy, strange . . . something."

Benton had an image of Gacy, the eyes of a psychotic in a clown's face.

"How was he dressed?"

"T-shirt, jeans, boots, leather jacket."

"And that van. You think it was his?"

"Yeah. It wasn't there when I came back with the police right after my father picked me up, so I think it was his."

"What'd it look like?"

"It was a 1978 Ford Econoline van, blue or black, and it had bodywork."

"How do you know?"

"I have five brothers, and for years outside our house looked like a used-car lot. The right front fender had been worked on or replaced—anyway it was primed."

"Did you happen to notice the license plate?"

"She shook her head. "I didn't get any number, but I know one thing: It was a New York State plate."

"Why's that?"

"It was that mustard color New York used to use until they changed to the Statue of Liberty plates."

"Good," Benton said. "You didn't notice any numbers, though?"

224

"No. I really couldn't see them."

It all fit, Benton thought, except her hair. He looked at it very closely.

"May I ask you a personal question?"

She nodded.

"Is that your natural hair color?"

"That's not personal," she said. "No. It's not. I'm a natural blond. I got an idea to dye my hair not long ago."

"How long ago?"

"Last Tuesday."

"You were a blonde when you were assaulted?"

"That's right."

Inside, something soared in Benton. This woman had seen the killer.

For a moment, the woman seemed reflective. "Any other questions?"

"Not now," Benton said. "But I'd like to take your number."

"No problem." She wrote her number on a card Benton gave her and handed it back.

She paused before going back into the store. "You know," she said, "when I thought about things later I got the creeps. He didn't seem to mind my seeing his van. I mean, maybe he intended doing more to me than what I thought. Maybe he really was going to murder me."

Benton looked at her. *There was no maybe about it,* he thought.

CHAPTER 33

An old-time homicide detective who had many dealings, with them once characterized the employees of the New York State Department of Motor Vehicles as "thousands of mean three-toed sloths. You couldn't get these fuckers to move," he said, "if the world was coming to an end."

Benton didn't find this exactly true. Nevertheless, even with his rabbi in Albany, where the main headquarters were located, it took three days to get a printout on all the 1978 Ford Econoline vans in the five boroughs of New York.

The real problem was the number: 5,678. That was busy-work of mountainous proportions. To some degree, he could whittle that number down—arbitrarily. He could make the assumption that the killer lived in the Bronx—because he seemed to know the area so well—which was another assumption.

That got it down to 234 vans.

Further, he could eliminate—arbitrarily again—all vans with commercial plates—though he felt a little squeamish doing this, too—and reduce the number to 103.

That wouldn't have been terribly bad, except Lawless had told him that he could only spare one person now: Barbara Babalino.

The hunt for the van was going to take a couple of weeks at least, and there was no guarantee that his arbitrary paring down of the list had not pared off the suspect van.

On the other hand, it was a lead. He had no choice but to follow it through and hope for the best.

The printout was arranged alphabetically. Barbara would cover owner's names beginning with the first thirteen letters of the alphabet and Benton the last thirteen.

They discussed what they might do if they came upon a suspect. Under no circumstances would they attempt to make a collar alone. That could be dangerous.

But, for the moment, Benton thought, that was dreaming.

Both detectives used pool cars, not wanting to park their own cars in streets of some of the precincts they would be visiting.

After he had tracked down the owners of ten of the vans, Benton was struck by one thing: almost half of them had been primed—gray—for a new paint job. There wasn't any particular explanation for this—it just was.

Most of the people Benton saw were Hispanic, though he did have one exciting moment when he met with a young guy who seemed to fit the physical requirements of the killer—he was blond and muscular and had a "jovial" face—and also owned a van that showed some bodywork on the front fender. It was the left front, but the woman in the store could have been mistaken.

But his hopes were dashed.

It turned out that the guy was a PO in the Five Two and he readily allowed Benton to confirm that he had been on the four-to-midnight tour on the day the woman had been assaulted.

All Benton could do was continue to track down owners, ever conscious that he was working against the clock.

Barbara had no luck either, but she was glad she had the experience she did as she found and interviewed van owners. A couple had hit on her, and she had to put them in their place quickly.

In her two days of canvassing she had seen fifteen owners. She would have seen seventeen, but two of them weren't in. She figured she would double back and check them out first chance she got.

One of them lived in a large old house on the corner of 198th Street and Valentine Avenue.

It was an unusual house because it was painted and in good condition on a block where most of the houses were either in disrepair or abandoned.

Barbara had wanted to talk to neighbors about the occupant and his van, but there were no neighbors. The houses directly across the street and flanking the house itself were abandoned.

She supposed it must be quite a person who would live in a house and take care of it on a block like this. His name, she noted, was Albert Brooks III. She would recheck him later.

She went on to the C's.

CHAPTER 34

Anne Bauman refused to be cowed by the punks in the neighborhood, the predators who sold crack and the junkies and assorted crazies that prowled the streets. If she was late, and the parking lot was filled, as it had been tonight, she would park on the street.

She wasn't particularly scared of the bad guys. In her pocketbook she carried an illegal but very effective spray can of Mace. If someone messed with her they would get that in their eyeballs.

Now, as she drove along Pelham Parkway West, she was not thinking about that. She was thinking about Jeff, her boyfriend, who had only recently moved into her apartment on Eastchester Road.

It really made her look forward to going home at night. No more having to think about when she would see Jeff next. There he would be, at home.

Tomorrow they would both be home—but only for a little while. They were going to eat out, then catch *Cats* on Broadway. She was looking forward to that.

She glanced in the rearview mirror preparatory to making a left onto Eastchester, then did a double take and felt her body go cold: another pair of eyes were in the rearview mirror, looking at her.

CHAPTER 35

For a moment, Benton didn't know where he was. Then he realized that he was home and it was sometime early in the morning.

The phone was ringing.

He reached over and picked it off the bedstand.

It was Lawless, and Benton was instantly awake.

"We got another, George," he said.

"Where?"

"Same place. St. Bonaventure."

"I'll be right there."

Benton hung up the phone.

God.

CHAPTER 36

This time, Benton got to the scene in about twenty minutes.

On the way, the things that had been festering and working on him enlarged. Christ, he felt so guilty that by the time he got to the scene—or the dump—he felt like *he* had done the girl.

It was eerily similar to the first scene: shelter half in place, blue-and-whites' lights revolving, crowd behind crime scene tape, Lawless and Babalino near the body, Edmunton and Piccolo working the crowd.

He came up to Lawless.

"Like you said, George," Lawless said.

Benton blinked. He felt very shaky, but he knew that it didn't show. Or at least he thought it didn't show. You spend your life acting, you get good at it.

The girl in the scrunched-up fetal position, just like the others.

She was smaller than Michelle Reynolds, but he had worked on her with ferocity—she was even more cut than Reynolds. Indeed, Benton thought she looked like she had been attacked by a wild animal.

He went through the motions, though he knew what they would find. Nothing. The killer was laughing at him. *What now, cop?*

Benton spent two hours at the scene, and then the wheels were put in motion, just as they had been before. Piccolo and Edmunton would try to ID the girl. The usual checks would be made.

Benton suggested, and Lawless accepted, the idea that a couple more cops would help him and Barbara in trying to run down the van.

Benton was glad. He had not felt capable of defending any position he took.

Then he left for home. He told Lawless he was going to take a short nap before hitting the van trail again.

Thank God Lawless didn't ask him if he was all right. He didn't like lying to Joe Lawless, but if he told him how badly shaken he felt he might take him off the case.

No, Lawless wouldn't do that.

Would he?

When he got home, Benton undressed to his shorts and carefully hung everything up. He laid his wadcutter on the bedstand in the bedroom.

He went into the bathroom and looked at himself in the mirror. It made him feel a little better. He was in the mirror; he existed.

He opened the cabinet doors.

His eyes flicked from left to right. Medications galore.

He could take any number of them. Then he thought humorlessly, *Bring on the* Titanic.

But for him the case would be over. He would not be able to think clearly enough.

He closed the doors and his face appeared again. He

looked like an ordinary human being: dark-haired, dark-eyed, good-looking, relatively few wrinkles.

It was hard to recognize himself in the mirror. The person who looked back at him was not the person he felt like inside.

He went to the bedroom and lay down.

He could feel the anxiety starting to build, and it scared him, fueled the fire, added more anxiety.

He felt his pulse. His heart rate had picked up. He started to breathe more quickly.

What was he? Who was he?

Nothing.

He remembered.

He was always so bizarre, so bent.

When he was a little kid on the block—they used to play in Central Park—and other kids would say bad things about his mother and father, he would make believe he didn't care. He did, but he wouldn't fight for them.

He was afraid.

He thought of the ninth victim, Adrienne Lowell. He saw the color photos. Jesus. She looked like she belonged in a butcher shop. This one too.

It was the same in grammar school, that exclusive Town and Country place where his mother and father had sent him to board—so he wouldn't get in their hair. The kids picked on him there, and he was always afraid to fight back.

He was missing something in the case. It was there. Something important. A clue. A lead. Had to be.

Baloney.

In high school he was picked on—and never did anything. And the girls he liked . . . Christ, he liked Angela DeBonno—she was beautiful—but he never said anything to her for all four years he was there, never said anything because he was afraid, afraid she wouldn't go out with him.

How he had ached for her.

He wondered where she was today.

He would chastise himself angrily. *Next time. I'll do this. I'll do that.*

But next time never came.

He thought of Kemper. How terrified he must have been, the son of a man who made him eat a pet. And Bianchi, waiting for the next time his mother burned his hand. And Armstrong, whose mother had never taken care of him.

Anxiety. That's what Benton had had all his fucking life. Vague, unexplainable, often severe.

How did he handle it?

Jerking off, medications, dreaming, fantasy . . . fantasy was the biggie.

When he was ten he was going to be a fireman, then a general, then a boxer, then a cop. Somebody strong, somebody who could handle things.

What things?

Life?

No, deeper than that. Had to be. Plenty of people handled life with no great amount of anxiety, so why couldn't he?

He smiled. Who knew?

Dr. Stern had explained the difference between anxiety and fear. Fear was logical and proper—you see a lion running at you it's appropriate to be afraid.

But anxiety, that was different. That was inappropriate.

"A schizophrenic," Stern had said, "can be just as afraid of a teddy bear as you are of a lion."

Anxiety, anxiety, anxiety . . .

You had to deal with it.

He looked at the gun. The hole in the barrel looked large. He fantasized sticking the barrel in his mouth and firing. Behind his head would be a frame, say 4 x 5, to catch the brain matter. Instant art.

Christ, he bet somebody would sell it.

That was another way to handle the anxiety.

Killing himself. Christ, that was so close to killing . . . that's what the doctors said, right? Suicide and homicide were bedfellows.

He felt his pulse. It was going at around a hundred beats a minute. He could feel a little constriction in his chest.

That meant he wasn't going to kill himself. Suicidal people are calm people. Why? All their problems are solved. It was when you were still fighting to survive that you were anxious.

Tears formed in his eyes. He thought of the little blond girl. The 7-Eleven girl. He couldn't help her anymore. She and others would die. That was too bad.

Suicide and homicide. Yes! Close. Some people handled their anxiety by suicide, others by homicide.

Control, right, smash it out. Serial murderers killed their past, murdered the things that threatened them. Yes, that was what they were doing: canceling out profound anxiety—temporarily, of course.

Yes, that was the fucking difference between him and a serial murderer. He fantasized suicide, they acted out homicide. The anxiety was the key. They had more, he had less. Their solutions were more intense, but the bottom line was that it was just a matter of degree.

He cackled in the stillness of the bedroom.

I am losing my fucking mind, he thought.

And where does the anxiety come from? The bog of your mind, "that undiscovered country from whose bourne no traveller returns." The unconscious. Buried there forever by people who don't love you and make you eat your pets and abandon you when you're five fucking years old and make you suck off men and burn your hands and abandon you and beat you and tell you you're a worthless piece of slime . . .

He laughed out loud again, and tears mixed with the laughter. It comes from somewhere in there.

He knew, then, that he could never be healthy. He was just like the serial murderer. They both were doomed to live their problems until they hit the mahogany.

Ha-ha.

He looked back at the gun.

He thought the blond girl in the 7-Eleven.

She will die again, he thought. Because they couldn't canvass fast enough to stop this guy. Even if they checked a hundred van owners, he would kill again.

Even if he could solve it, there would be a temporary high, and then he would return to this. He was fatally injured in his youth; it had taken a long time for him to die.

Tears rolled down the sides of his face.

He felt his pulse. His heartbeat was receding. He was getting calmer.

"I am," he said, "running out of hope. I am a dangerous man. A man without hope is one bad motherfucker."

He blinked.

If I die, the 7-Eleven girl will die with me. Lawless can't do it, Babalino can't . . . as bad as I feel I believe I have a better shot of collaring him than they. *There is no joy in this*, he thought, *just perceived fact.*

That girl and other girls have a right to live. They are so young, they smell so good, they are so beautiful and innocent.

He sat up on the edge of the bed. He felt rage boiling up.

I have to put all this shit behind me, he thought, *put it in a place where it doesn't affect me and go and run this fucker to ground.*

Later, when it's over, then maybe we'll see what we're going to do. But now, now is the time to give it everything I have.

For you, kid, and he smiled. He pictured Humphrey Bogart at the airport saying good-bye to Ingrid Bergman in *Casablanca*.

He smiled.

Christ, he was out to lunch.

CHAPTER 37

The ring, Albert thought, would solve everything.

He had been going out with Ellen nine months now. It was great in the beginning, but over the last couple of months he had sensed a change in her. She seemed to find fault with everything he did.

"Oh, Albert," she had told him when they were out the previous week, "you're always saying that you're going to do this, that, and the other thing. But you haven't done anything. You're still in a dead-end job. You just have no sense of responsibility. You're becoming a figment of your own imagination."

If Ellen had seen what Albert was feeling she would have been scared. But Albert didn't show it, and after a while the bad feelings went away.

He did love her. Yes. She was the only girl he had ever loved in his whole life. He, of course, had had plenty of opportunity to go out with girls in high school and later, but he chose not to.

But Ellen was special. A special sweet dark-haired person who did strange things to his stomach.

She was a little young, only twenty, but she was very mature and sure of herself. She was a junior at Mount St. Vincent's majoring in business, and he thought she would go places someday.

He had met her at a school dance that he went to there. He wanted to meet new people, people more in keeping with his own sense of inner worth, which was quite high. The people at work were a bunch of assholes.

So he went to the dance, at Mount St. Vincent's, and told everyone he met that he was a student at Manhattan College. Since he had some experience with it, no one questioned him.

He and Ellen had been attracted to one another immediately. Albert was smart, pleasant-looking, and very appealing to women. He could remember the look in Ellen's eyes the first day they went to the beach and she saw him in his bathing trunks.

Sparks flew.

She never found out that he didn't go to Manhattan. He just told her that he had quit for a while to earn some money. He made it sound like he was very responsible.

Indeed, he never told her anything about himself, and she, at first, didn't question him closely.

That was good, because she might have wondered why he had been thrown out of four different colleges and two high schools.

And if she went back further, she would have seen that he had been to court twice for arson and once for extreme cruelty to animals.

Albert had put together a scenario of how it would be, and it had a very happy ending. He would marry Ellen, go back to college, get a great job, and have a lot of money and power—which was only right—and they would have kids and live happily ever after.

Things that bothered him from the past, all those unhappy memories, he could just blot them out, make believe they didn't happen.

Ellen's action a month ago, when she told him she would rather not have sex for a while, really bothered him. He didn't realize how much until someone on the job remarked that he looked like he needed some sleep, and he realized that, basically, he had not slept for seventy hours since she had stopped the sex.

He didn't want to think about not being with her. It made him go cold and hollow inside; the thoughts were intolerable.

But now, as he headed for her apartment, which was on 207th Street and Broadway, he knew he had the solution. He had bought her an expensive ring—she didn't have to know the money came from some stuff he had shoplifted and sold—and he would give it to her, and ask her to be his wife.

He would start the new year with the prospect of a new life.

That would show her, in one fell swoop, how responsible he was. And he would also tell her that he was going back to college. She would have nothing to complain about.

She lived downstairs in a private home, and when he rang the bell three times and she didn't answer, he was disappointed. He should have called before he came over, but he wanted it to be a wonderful surprise.

He started to leave. He figured he would call her

and leave word on her answering machine for her to call him.

He was almost to his van when he heard a thick, Yiddish voice behind him.

"Mister?"

He turned. A fat old lady was coming down the porch steps. It was Ellen's landlady.

"Vait a minute."

She came up to him, huffing and puffing. "You Albert, right?"

"Yes."

"Ellen left this for you before she left."

Something pierced Albert. "Left?"

"She moved out yesterday."

Albert opened and read the note in the van. For some reason he didn't want anyone to see him reading it. It had to be bad.

It was.

Dearest Albert,

I have enjoyed our relationship over the past nine months, but now I am sad to say it must end. It isn't you. You're great. But it's just that as fate would have it I met someone else. I will always remember you, Albert, and thanks for a wonderful time.

Good luck in all your future endeavors.

Sincerely,
Ellen

Tears rolled down his face, and then something started to scream inside his head.

If you asked him, he wouldn't have been able to tell you

how he got to Long Branch the next day. But there he was.

He probably wouldn't have heard you anyway. Most of his time was spent talking with Ray.

CHAPTER 38

Benton worked until eleven o'clock at night on the day the new body was discovered. Then he went home, exhausted.

He had a nightmare of a kind that was not unusual for him.

In the nightmare, there was a light-haired killer doing something, and at first Benton couldn't do anything because he was completely sealed in a glass tube.

Then he saw.

The killer was laughing as he built a house of human bones. There was a truck backed up to the site, the ground was bloodred, and on it the house was being framed out.

It was horrendous and pathetic and scary at the same time.

Benton screamed and screamed and screamed and could do nothing . . . until the glass broke. Then there was the killer, turning to him as he heard George Benton's scream shatter the stillness.

Benton woke up screaming, and for a moment he didn't know where he was. Then he realized: in his room, alone in the dark. And then . . . and then the word occurred, and it was like something that he had known for as long as he existed. Why didn't he realize it before?

Construction. The key, the link, oh Jesus, yes, it had to be.

He was now fully awake. He didn't need any notes to tell him what he wanted to know.

Holmdel, Freehold, Jacobi, Parsippany, Staten Island— every single one of them had construction going on or recently finished. Interior work. That was a little unusual, wasn't it? All five places had work crews inside. Maybe one of those workmen was in all five places.

He went into the bathroom and splashed cold water on his face.

It was five o'clock. He pondered calling Lawless. No. Run it down first.

At eight o'clock, he began his phone calls.

People who spoke to him at the data processing firm in Parsippany said someone would get back to him; the same with the College of Staten Island.

But with those he got through to it was the same old fucking story—no one knew anything.

By twelve o'clock the news he had gotten was disappointing.

The maintenance people at Freehold said that construction had been going on all year with all kinds of companies, and Holmdel said the same thing.

His theory was starting to take a little water.

The guy from Jacobi got back to him at three o'clock. "We were mainly having new wire installed," he said. And then Benton remembered: a number of the places were getting or had gotten new wiring.

"What was the name of the company?"

"Wizard Electric."

"Do you know where they're based?"

"The Bronx. They have a big shop up on Bailey Avenue."

Benton called back the Freehold maintenance guy.

Benton's heart rate escalated when the man told Benton that Wizard Electric from the Bronx had done the work there. They had installed a lot of new communications wire.

He got through to the Holmdel guy at three forty-five. It was like checking a chest X-ray when you've smoked for fifty years and have a cough that sounds like a chest of china falling.

"Wizard Electric," he said. "Toward the end of April and early May they were down here."

Rosalinde Berne's body had been found May 1.

Nail it to the wall, he thought. He called Monmouth College, where the first victim—Julia Schmitt—had come from. He identified himself and got through to the VP.

"Yes, we had this place rewired—it's very old—in December of 1986."

"Do you remember the name of the company that did the job?"

"Sure. Wizard Electric."

Benton looked them up in the book and dialed the number. He breathed deeply while he waited.

The phone rang for a long time, and what sounded like an answering service responded.

"Is anyone there from the company?" he asked the woman who had answered.

"I don't know. Just a minute. Who's this?"

"I'm a police officer."

246

Ten seconds later, another woman came on the line. "May I help you?"

"Yes, I'm trying to locate someone who works for you. He drives a van, an Econoline van."

"I'm sorry, I can't give out any information."

"Can you give me the number of someone who can?"

"I don't know."

"Otherwise I'll have to get a court order."

Pause. "All right."

She gave him the number of Joe Robinson, the executive VP.

He called the number. A little kid came on the phone.

"Mr. Robinson, please."

A moment later, a husky-voiced man said hello.

Benton made it brief. "Mr. Robinson, I'm Detective George Benton with the Fifty-third Precinct in the Bronx. I have to talk to you in confidence and very quickly about someone who is possibly one of your employees."

"Who?"

"I'll tell you when I see you."

Benton made arrangements to meet with Robinson, who lived in Mineola, Long Island, right away.

A minute after he hung up he was burning rubber up the block.

CHAPTER 39

Robinson lived in an apartment house. By the time Benton got there it was dark. Dark and cold.

They went into the room that Robinson used as an office. It was a pleasant room and obviously the domain of a man into things technical. Robinson had some engineering stuff made into art objects and mounted on little pedestals.

Benton had no idea what they were.

"How can I help you?"

"Do you have an employee who drives an Econoline van?"

Robinson nodded. "Albert Brooks drives an Econoline."

"Is it . . . I mean, has it had bodywork done on it recently?"

"Yeah. Fender. Front. What's this about?"

"He might have used the van in the commission of a crime." Benton said it flatly, but inside he was yelping with joy, vibrating with excitement.

"What?"

"I'm not at liberty to say. Can you tell me what he looks like?"

"About six feet. Wiry. Blondish hair. Big ears. He's got a funny face."

"How much you know about him?"

"Not much. Guys like him come and go. He's a wire puller."

"What's that?"

"Low man on the technical pole. It's his job to pull wires through the ceiling from closet to closet."

"Closet to closet . . . ?"

"Telephone closet to telephone closet. It's bullwork. No real skill required."

"How long has he been with you?"

"I don't know exactly, but at least a year."

"I'm going to mention a series of places. Will you tell me if you've had any jobs there over the last nine months?"

Benton mentioned all of the places where the bodies had been found.

Wizard Electric had been at every place except Staten Island and Old Bridge.

"One thing I don't understand," Benton said. "You're a Bronx firm. Why do you work in Jersey?"

"You go where the work is. We get a lot of work from big companies like AT&T, who would find it too expensive to do certain jobs."

"So you commute there."

"Sometimes. Sometimes if the job is far, we give the men a per diem for renting a room."

Benton nodded. "Let me ask you. What kind of a person is Albert Brooks?"

"I couldn't tell you," Robinson said. "I don't really know him. He seems like a good guy. He works hard."

"Thanks for your help," Benton said. "And this is between us, right?"

"No problem," Robinson said. "But I would appreciate finding out what this is all about soon. I don't want a guy working for me if he's a thief or something. Is he an ex-con?"

"No," Benton said. He paused. "One other question. Where does he live?"

Robinson got up, went over to a desk, and picked up a small metal file box. He handed a card to Benton: 1870 Valentine Avenue, Bronx, New York.

Thirty seconds later Benton was gone.

CHAPTER 40

Benton drove back to the Bronx at high speed. He figured the best thing to do was to go to the precinct. Then they could set up a plan for a stakeout, or assault, whatever Lawless said.

Benton was sky-high and just yesterday he had felt like a dog. It was the case of course. It was solved. All that was left was the collar, getting his picture taken for newspapers, the compliments of other cops. He felt important.

An errant thought, which he knew was true: It wouldn't last.

In the past when a case had not gone well he had felt bad—but not like yesterday. Christ, he'd been toying with the idea of eating his wadcutter.

The anxiety, the shit, had invaded an area that was as solid as anything he had: his sense of worth as a cop. Christ, couldn't he just say, Yes, you're a good detective, and you win some and lose some. Does everything have to be life and death?

Christ.

And this killer. What about him? What would he do without someone to kill! That would bother him no end.

Benton tooled across the Throg's Neck Bridge. The Bronx spread out in front of him and, far down to the south, the magic show on the Hudson, New York.

He paid his toll and went through.

He thought about the little 7-Eleven girl.

He should have radioed ahead. But he was in his BMW. He had no radio. Why had he done that?

Maybe he'd planned it that way.

Planned for what?

A question: What if right now this guy was heading back to his house with live prey in the van?

They would plan the assault, plan the collar, and it wouldn't save a life.

He sped along the Cross Bronx Expressway. He would get off at Webster to get to the precinct.

The Webster Avenue exit loomed. It was no contest.

He stayed on, and got off at Jerome Avenue. It was not the way to the station house.

Benton had figured on calling from a public phone when he got to Valentine. But there were no phones in sight.

There was no van in sight either.

The street was typical Fort Siberia: decaying, the remnants of some wonderful yesterdays—and some not so wonderful yesterdays—enshrined in the buildings.

The house had no lights on. Indeed, there were only a few houses on the entire street where he could see lights. The street was dying in the darkness.

What a sad way to go, Benton thought.

252

He parked four or five houses down and walked toward the house.

He was aware of his wadcutter. He remembered Albert Fish.

Beware.

His heart beat faster, and something deep inside told him to go back.

He couldn't.

He stood in front of the house. There was no sign of life inside.

He debated for a moment, then went back to his car and took out a cat's-paw and flashlight.

He was compelled to go inside. It was illegal. Fuck it.

He went down an alleyway that ran between an abandoned house and the suspect house.

The back area had a garden, fairly well tended, and a patio that loomed up before him.

There was a sun porch with what looked like a flimsy door.

A minute later he was inside the sun porch, and then inside the door of the house itself. It was totally black. He listened before going further. Not a sound.

He turned the flashlight on.

He was in the living room—and it was like from another time.

The furniture and furnishings were old, maybe from the forties, but well kept.

Time had stopped in this room forty years ago.

Beneath the tenseness he felt a surge of sadness.

He went upstairs.

All the rooms were empty.

He went downstairs. These rooms were also empty, except for the living room, a kitchen which was recently used, and one bedroom, which had an old brass bedstead, chifforobe, and trunk.

He felt the bed. Dust glittered in the rays of the flashlight.

No one had slept in this bed for many years.

He shuddered, aware that he was sweating. What the fuck was he doing here? He should radio this in, get an ESD team here.

He realized that he was in the presence of madness.

It was dangerous.

Benton, compelled, found the door to the basement and went down.

He immediately smelled body odor. Like a gym. Somebody worked out down here.

At the foot of the stairs he played his light around the basement. He saw a mat, barbells, a freezer in one corner, a closet, and a cot.

Nothing else, but somebody lived down here. And did God knew what else.

The furnace went on, startling him. It roared as he approached the closet.

He opened it, flashlight in one hand, the other on his wadcutter.

The door creaked. Why fucking not? Some clothes on shelves, brightly colored.

Down in a corner, a stuffed animal. He picked it up. An old, battered teddy bear.

None of the victims had been young. He wondered who it belonged to.

He picked up a handful of the clothing.

Sweet Jesus.

Bras, panties, shoes, other garments.

He looked closer and froze. Many of the items were stained with dried blood.

Good Christ! It looked like enough to stock a shop.

His trophies of the hunt.

How sad for these people.

There was a wooden box on the floor. He pulled the lid off, and the smell hit him. The smell of dried blood. In the box was an ax and a knife, both with dried blood.

Benton heard a sound. The growl of a truck. On the street.

He flicked off the light, raced upstairs, and looked out a window.

In the darkness he saw the outline of an Econoline.

Now it was too late to call. *Now it's me and him, which is the way you wanted it, right, you compulsive fucker?*

But he was not afraid.

He went out the back door the way he had come, then up the alley.

The man had exited the truck and was walking toward the house.

Benton stepped out and shone the flashlight in his eyes, his wadcutter ready.

"Albert Brooks?"

"Yes."

"You're under arrest."

"Why? I didn't do anything," he said. He had a soft, pleasant voice.

"Lie on your belly and put your arms behind your back."

"Okay. Okay. Take it easy."

Brooks lay on the street and put his arms behind his back.

Benton extinguished the flashlight.

This was a cuffing a perp mano-a-mano, a very dangerous enterprise.

Benton knew he had to be careful.

He took his cuffs off his belt, keeping the wadcutter at the ready.

He got one cuff on and almost the other, and the action was so fast and catlike that he didn't even see it coming. Then George Benton knew that he was in a fight for his life.

Brooks was on his feet, and he had George's gun hand gripped so hard it almost made George yelp with pain, and George had Brooks's arm gripped. In it was a wire, a thin wire.

It was no contest.

Within a minute, the wadcutter had clattered out of Benton's hand and Brooks was straddling him. The wire was around his neck, and Brooks was tightening it, and Benton realized he was going to die.

If he had unconsciously wanted to die, he was being accommodated.

Brooks looked down at him, his eyes glittering insanely.

Benton had one hope: his four-shot derringer in the ankle holster. He bore down, trying to absorb the pain, fighting his failing consciousness, trying to pull the wire away from his neck while allowing his other hand to get to his leg, which he twisted awkwardly, almost beyond the breaking point.

And then he grabbed the gun and squeezed the trigger just as the blackness closed down around him.

EPILOGUE

George Benton didn't even have to spend any time in the hospital. He had lost and regained consciousness almost immediately, and had discovered that Albert Brooks III was lying dead on top of him.

Benton had only succeeded in shooting Brooks in the leg, but it had shattered the femur—a compound fracture—and lacerated the femoral artery. Stunned and in pain, Brooks had rapidly bled to death.

As Benton had expected, he was feted.

Lawless, Babalino, and the entire crew took him to a joint on 116th Street and Pleasant Avenue, and they celebrated to the wee hours. Benton allowed himself some wine and got mildly shitfaced.

It took a couple of weeks to close down the investigation.

Though it could never be confirmed, it was determined that Albert Brooks had mainly killed the girls at various sites, then had transported their bodies to his cellar, where he worked on them.

There might have been a couple of instances when he had taken them into the cellar still alive.

Dried blood was found at the edges of the tile floor, and in some of the seams.

Identities of the remains in the freezer were determined, as far as possible, and returned to their loved ones.

The house was owned by Albert Brooks III, who had purchased it from the city two years earlier. A check of the records indicated that it was first owned by his relatives and his mother, who then sold it to another family. It went through the hands of a few more families before it was seized for back taxes by the city and reclaimed by Albert.

An attempt was made to contact Albert's mother, Bobby Jo Brooks, but it was unsuccessful.

Benton couldn't help but wonder why Albert had gotten it back. Why did he return to the place where he had been raised? Maybe to look for the something that couldn't have been there in the first place.

It was all so crazy.

Benton had one other question that would go unanswered. Why had the girls been arranged in a fetal position? He thought he had the beginning of an answer: because then they were like babies, and then he could control them. Wasn't controlling anxiety, disabling the threat—though a threat that only existed in his head—the reason behind all of Brooks's actions?

Albert Brooks was buried in potter's field four days after he was killed. A small service was held in the chapel on the grounds, and there was only one person who paid his respects: George Benton.

He knew, of course, that Albert Brooks's—story had to have a unhappy ending, and he told himself that he was a monster who had to die so that others might live, but there he was. He mourned Albert Brooks III.

The Bent One.

And how, he thought now, *will my story end?*

It was a Monday morning two weeks to the day after Albert Brooks was killed, and Benton was walking north along Fifth Avenue at 85th Street. Christmas decorations were up, there was a hint of snow, and there was a certain festiveness in the air that was pure New York City.

To his left was Central Park, playground of his youth, where he dreamed his dreams and fantasized that it would all have a happy ending.

He still believed it could, though it might take some doing. And it would be a different kind of happy.

Oh, yeah.

At 87th Street he turned and walked east, and as he did the anxiety, that old and unwelcome companion, started to come at him with determination. It had awakened him a couple of times during the night. If he wanted to do what he was going to do, he would pay a price.

Ahead, the building loomed, and people on the street seemed to look at him and say, *You are a sick fucker, a sickee, you are different from all of us.*

But that wasn't true. That was just a trick of the mind.

Five yards from the entrance the anxiety really rocked him. A voice inside whispered to him to stop. . . .

Something told him to keep going.

He turned into the entrance. He walked across a well-appointed hall to the elevator and stood there.

Thirty seconds later he was on the second floor, walking down a quiet hallway to a door at the far end.

He stood in front of the door.

It was crunch time.

He watched his finger press the bell.

Fifteen seconds later the door opened. Standing in the doorway was a small, white-haired man. He was smiling.

"Dr. Stern," Benton said. "How are you?"

"Fine. I'm so very glad you could make it."

THE SNOW BEES
Peter Cunningham

Patrick Drake is ambitious. He's a high flyer who wants to get to the top of the corporate ladder – fast. And a business trip to sort out a fiasco of a French vineyard looks just like the fast track to promotion.

It isn't. He reports back to head office and then he's fired.

From muck-raking in a molehill of missing money, he steps on a minefield of murderous activity. In a tightening web of terrorism and violence he finds himself facing the naked savagery of the international cocaine trade. Fighting to clear his name – and to save his life – he unravels a thread of fear and fanaticism that runs from South Africa to Spain, from Ireland to the United States. And at any moment he may feel the fatal sting . . .

'Ripping' *Oxford Times*
'Gripping' *Standard*

0 7474 0137 3
THRILLER

All Sphere Books are available at your bookshop or
newsagent, or can be ordered from the following address:
Sphere Books, Cash Sales Department, P.O. Box 11,
Falmouth, Cornwall TR10 9EN.

Please send cheque or postal order (no currency), and
allow 60p for postage and packing for the first book plus
25p for the second book and 15p for each additional book
ordered up to a maximum charge of £1.90 in U.K.

B.F.P.O. customers please allow 60p for the first book, 25p
for the second book plus 15p per copy for the next 7 books,
thereafter 9p per book.

Overseas customers, including Eire, please allow £1.25 for
postage and packing for the first book, 75p for the second
book and 28p for each subsequent title ordered.